Off the Wall Stories

Volume 2

Off the Wall Stories
Volume 2

by

Al Stevens

This book is a work of fiction. The people in this book are fictional. Any resemblance to any real person, living or dead, is coincidental.

Mockingbird Songs & Stories, Cocoa, FL

Dedication

To the fond memory of David and Susan Dunscombe

Table of Contents

Preface

In the late 1980s, I was alone on an extended business trip to a place where I did not speak the native tongue. Lonely, knowing no one, and with nothing to do, I set up my luggable, portable computer in the hotel room and began to write stories drawn from my personal and professional experience.

All of which explains why some of these stories are outdated. They deal with thirty-year-old computer technology and social issues. They predate the Internet, social media, and cell phones.

Rather than upgrade and rewrite those old stories, I am publishing them as I first wrote them with minor corrections here and there and perhaps a touch of rewrite where needed.

I published the first volume of this work, *Off the Wall Stories*, in 2012, with stories I'd written since retiring, most of which are not related to technology. The old stories in this second volume didn't make that cut because of their obsolete technical content. When I decided to do this volume, I gathered up the neglected stories and added a few more for a second collection, which you are now reading.

Al Stevens, 2020

Death in Rehab

The cart's wheels squeaked and chattered as they rolled down the tiled corridor. Nurse Walt Pullen pushed it along, using the bulk of his small frame to propel the cart, heading back to the second floor nurses' station, and in no hurry. His evening rounds over, the fortyish nurse could return, catch up on paperwork, and then sit at his desk, reading his paperback novel, on call in case a patient buzzed for assistance. He'd done this same work for years, pushing carts, dispensing meds, and waiting for buzzers, years spent mostly indoors with a pallor of a complexion and a small paunch to show for it.

As he rolled along, he thought about the future. They had announced that the rehab center would be closed in the coming year. Something about real estate values. It would mean he'd have to find another job, not an easy matter for a male nurse his age. The irony amused him. The facility's owner was now one of its patients, a stroke survivor in the room he was rolling past. Pullen didn't wish a stroke on anyone, but maybe this guy's stay here would convince him of the need to keep the place open. Or maybe he'd die and his heirs would want to keep it going. Pullen could only hope.

He wheeled his cart past Mr. Clark's room, lost in his thoughts. A loud report like a backfire came from inside. Pullen stopped pushing, stepped to the door, and gave it a yank. It wouldn't open. Something inside had it jammed shut. The harder he pulled, the more the door resisted.

He punched a button on his mobile intercom. A sluggish voice answered, "Dempsey here."

"This is Pullen. I'm on the second floor. Sounded like a gunshot from Mr. Clark's room, and I can't get the door open."

"Be right there."

Pullen paced back and forth, checking his watch. This was a first for him. In twenty years on this job, he'd never heard a gunshot. He worried that somehow he'd be found at blame. He wished Dempsey would get there.

After a few minutes, Bob Dempsey stepped out of the elevator at the end of the hall, his uniform rumpled as if he'd slept in it, which he probably had. He adjusted his holster and ran his fingers through the wisp of grey hair that surrounded his bald spot. He walked briskly from the elevator toward the room.

Fester Walton trailed along behind, carrying his toolbox, which clattered in time with his steps. Fester was the resident maintenance man. His job was both indoors and out, he'd been at it since a young man, and he had the ruddy complexion, callused hands, and stooped shoulders to prove it.

They walked with urgency to where Pullen waited. Dempsey moved past Pullen without a word and gave the door a tug. It didn't budge. Walton tried it. Nothing. Patients' doors had no locks and opened into the hallway, so nothing should have prevented it from opening.

"Something's jammed in there," Dempsey said.

Walton gave it a pull. "Yep," he said. "Jammed."

"Well," Nurse Pullen said, "we have to get it open." There'd be hell to pay if something was wrong and they didn't get to Mr. Clark in time.

All three men nodded their understanding of the urgency of what Pullen suggested. Wilson Clark was a big shot in the community that was home to the Clarkton Rehabilitation Center. The town had been named after his ancestors, settlers from two centuries back, and his family had controlled most everything ever since. He was in his early seventies and owned a manufacturing plant, two restaurants, the newspaper, the hardware store, a television station, and other businesses that nobody seemed to know much about. Most of the working citizenry were in his employ one way or another. He'd come to the rehab center a month ago following a stroke. He occupied one of the few private rooms and kept the staff jumping during the day.

Walton pulled a hammer and screwdriver from his toolbox and punched out the hinge pins. The door fell slightly inward and rested against its frame. They maneuvered it down and twisted and pushed it in, knocking over a straight-backed chair that had been hanging from the doorknob on the other side of the door.

The three men climbed over the door and chair and pushed their way into the room. Pullen threw the light switch, but the overhead fluorescent light did not come on. When Walton shined his flashlight toward the bed, the three men fell back. Pullen was surprised and unnerved by what they found and the others seemed to be so too.

Wilson Clark, the town's leading citizen, was sitting up in bed, motionless, a small, round bloody wound on his left temple, his eyes wide open. A revolver lay on the bed next to Clark's left side. The room smelled of a mixture of antiseptic cleanser and spent gunpowder.

Pullen stepped over to the bed, pressed his fingers on the old man's neck, and felt for a pulse. He shook his head and looked at the other two men who stood staring at the dead man, their jaws open, their eyes wide. Dead old people were an uncommon sight at a rehab center, but it did happen occasionally. Dead old people with gunshot wounds were another matter altogether.

Dempsey snapped out of it and took charge. "Okay, everybody out of here. Don't touch anything. Go back to where you belong and wait."

He unclipped his cell phone from his belt and called 911. "This is Dempsey, security at Clarkton Rehab. There's been a shooting. Looks like suicide. Send the police and an ambulance."

Nurse Pullen went into the corridor and wondered what he should do. The shift paperwork needed attention, and regulations required him to complete and file the reports on time. But somebody would surely expect him to stay here and give his statement to the police. He didn't know which choice would get him in the most trouble. He decided to do his job as usual. They couldn't chew him out for that. He rolled the cart away from the scene and toward the nursing station.

***

Detective Emory Pfalzgraf stood at the unhinged, toppled door, which rested half against an overturned chair and half on the floor just inside the room. He shined his light around the room, and took careful measure of the scene.

A short bulky man in his early forties, Pfalzgraf wore a rumpled light-weight zip-up jacket over a plaid cotton shirt, blue jeans, and dirty running shoes without socks. The dress code didn't apply when you were pulled out of bed in the middle of the night, or so Pfalzgraf would rationalize if anyone asked. Didn't matter, though. The brass were all tucked in and comfy at home, not having had their sleep disturbed, and there was no one around to disapprove of his appearance. He ran his tongue over his teeth. He had neglected to brush in his haste to get dressed and to the scene. His mouth felt like the bottom of a bird cage.

This was a do-or-die case. Pfalzgraf was out of favor. His most recent case had been commandeered by the FBI and the brass didn't like having to turn over their hard-earned evidence to the Feebs who grabbed all the glory when the case was cracked. The bosses had given Phalzgraf an ultimatum: Close the next one yourself or start thinking about retirement.

Dempsey stood next to him, wringing his hands. "Never had anything like this happen before," he said.

Pfalzgraf ignored him. The detective was tired and looked it. Although he was accustomed to being rousted at all hours, he didn't much like it. But he was the town's only homicide detective, and he took his work seriously. When they called, he responded. Not as a reaction to the current instability of his position on the force but because he believed in advocating for those whose lives had ended unnecessarily.

"What do we have here?" he asked the uniformed cop standing guard at the door.

"I'm guessing a suicide," the uniform said. "That's what the E.M.T. thought when he declared him."

"The M.E. makes that call," Pfalzgraf said. "Let's see if we can guess." He turned to Dempsey. "Who found him?"

"Nurse Pullen heard the shot."

"Where's she?"

"He. He should be at the nursing station."

Pfalzgraf examined the body and its surroundings. What's this?" he asked.

"That's the tray the nurse brings him his meds on."

There were no pills on the tray, and the glass of water was half empty.

Based on what he saw, his gut instinct told him this was no suicide. The dead man was sitting up in bed with a bullet in his brain. Why does a guy take his meds just before he kills himself?

Pfalzgraf looked up at the overhead fluorescent light fixture. He stepped around the unhinged door to the wall switch by the doorway and shined his light on it. It was in the up position, indicating that the light was supposed to be on. He stretched a surgical glove onto his right hand and flipped the switch down and up. The light didn't work. "Mr. Dempsey," he said, "how long has that light been burnt out?"

"Not long," Dempsey said. "We stay on top of things like that."

"Why's the door off its hinges?"

"Couldn't get it open. I think that chair was wedged in it. Maybe the old man didn't want to be interrupted. Walton—he's our maintenance man—he knocked the hinge pins out."

"Who was first one inside?"

"We went in together," Dempsey said. "Three of us."

Pfalzgraf took a small digital camera from his jacket pocket and took pictures of everything. "Is there another room laid out like this one?" He wanted to reconstruct the scene without disturbing anything, and a similar room would allow him to do that.

Dempsey stepped into the light coming from the hallway, punched something into his cell phone, waited a few seconds, and said, "Next door. Vacant."

"You can tell that from your phone?" Pfalzgraf asked.

"It controls the security system. It's got a floor plan and who's in what rooms. Saves time."

"What'll they think of next?" Pfalzgraf said. He called out to one of the uniforms. "Come in here, climb on that chair, and check the tubes. But don't leave prints. Come on, Dempsey. Let's go look at that room."

They stepped out over the door and went a few steps down the corridor and into the adjacent room. It did have the same layout and furniture as the neighboring death scene. Pfalzgraf closed the door and wedged the back of the chair over the doorknob. Sure enough, the door wouldn't open. Then he removed the chair, positioned it under the light fixture, and stood on it.

"Yeah, I can reach the lights," he said as if to explain to Dempsey what he was doing. "Let's go back."

As they walked back to the scene, Pfalzgraf said, "Word's out they're closing this place."

"Yeah," Dempsey said, "That's the scuttlebutt."

"What happens to the people that work here?"

"I guess we look for jobs. Mr. Clark—the dead guy—would be making that decision. I guess not now."

When they returned to the scene, the overhead light was burning bright.

"One of the tubes was twisted out of its socket," said the uniformed cop.

Pfalzgraf grinned at Dempsey as if to say, "Told you." He looked at the ceiling again. "Replace the tube and take that one for evidence." He turned to Dempsey. "Get that nurse up here. And the maintenance man."

Dempsey made a couple calls, and a few minutes later, Pullen showed up followed by Walton lugging his toolbox. Dempsey introduced them.

"Tell me what happened," Pfalzgraf said.

Pullen told him the story as he said he remembered it. Walton nodded in agreement at the parts that included him.

"When's the last time you saw Mr. Clark alive?" Pfalzgraf asked Pullen.

"About ten minutes before. For his evening pills."

"You sure about the time?"

"Pretty much. You can check the surveillance videos."

Pfalzgraf jotted a note in his notepad. "Did you see a gun?"

"No, sir. I'd have reported that right away."

"Did the lights work?"

"Yes."

"What happened next?"

"I left him his pills like always right there on the tray."

Pfalzgraf paused and stood still for a moment. Then, "Did he need help with his pills?"

"No. He could feed himself and handle a cup okay."

"Do you watch to make sure the patients take their pills?"

"Not if they can do it themselves. I put the pills and some water on the nightstand. When I left, he was taking them."

Pfalzgraf made more notes. "Did you turn off the lights?"

"Yes, sir."

"And did you close the door?"

"Yes, sir. Mr. Clark was partial to his privacy."

"And later, did the lights work after you heard the shot?"

"No, sir. When we went in, they didn't. I figured one had burned out. One tube goes out, they both don't work. Walton here had a flashlight, and we used that."

Walton took his flashlight from his utility belt and showed it to everyone.

Pfalzgraf looked at the light switch, now in its up position with the light burning. "So, let's see if I got this right. After you left him alone, he gets out of bed, climbs on the chair, and twists the tube out of its socket. He gets down, hangs the chair on the door knob so nobody can open it, gets his gun from wherever, climbs in bed, and shoots himself. You think he could have done all that in the time he had?"

"No, sir. No way." Pullen shook his head. "Mr. Clark was paralyzed on one side. He needed help just going to the bathroom."

Pfalzgraf jotted something down. "And if he could have gotten up, why would he have wanted the lights to stay off?"

"I couldn't say."

"And why would he care whether anyone came in after he was dead?"

"Don't know that either," Pullen said. "Sometimes old folks get dementia after a stroke. No accounting for what they do. Or why."

"You say he was paralyzed? How?"

"His arm and leg."

"Which side?"

"Uh, let's see." Pullen turned himself as if to take the patient's position. "Left side."

Pfalzgraf looked again at the dead man, still sitting where they'd found him. "This was not suicide. This man was murdered."

The three men looked at each other and at Pfalzgraf.

"How?" Dempsey said. "Nobody was here when we broke in. Isn't that right, Pullen?"

"That's right," Pullen said, "and that door's the only way in or out."

"That's right," Walton said. "The only way."

Pfalzgraf nodded toward the bathroom and closet. "Anybody look in either of them?"

"No sir," Pullen said. "Dempsey told us not to touch anything."

"I did," said the uniform. "There's nobody in there."

Pfalzgraf opened the doors and peered in. Then he snorted. "Get everybody out and tape it off. This is a crime scene. Get prints off everything. Take the gun, the light tube, and the chair to the lab, and, of course, the body. And get that door out of the way."

Walton scrambled to move the door from in front of the doorway so they could move in and out without having to climb over it.

"Can I re-hang it?" he asked.

"Later when we're done," Pfalzgraf said, and he and Dempsey went out into the hallway. Pullen asked permission to leave and did so to return to his post. The detective looked up at two surveillance cameras, one at either end of the hall, and said, "Those things work?"

"Yes, sir. Two in every corridor, one at each end."

"They have audio?"

"No," Dempsey said. "We can watch but we can't listen."

"Yeah," Pfalzgraf said. "I knew that. Any other cameras?"

"One in the lobby."

"In the rooms, too?"

"No, sir. We can't. Privacy."

"I'll need those tapes."

"No tapes, sir. It's all on the computer."

Pfalzgraf stroked his chin and contemplated. "Okay. I'll need copies of the videos, visitor logs, employee time cards, any other records about comings and goings. You might as well start getting all that stuff together." He turned to the uniforms, "One of you go with Mr. Dempsey and stand by the computer until the warrants get here. Make sure nothing gets changed."

"Yes, sir."

Dempsey looked offended. "I wouldn't change anything."

"I don't think you would," Pfalzgraf said. "But we go by the book. Chain of custody. The deceased have family?"

"Only a nephew that I know of. He drops in about twice a week, usually in the evenings. We often talk."

"What about?"

"My job, mostly. He works with computers and said he's interested in the computer angle of security work. He showed me how to get inside the computer and look at the code. His uncle's company installed the security system."

***

Pfalzgraf sat at his desk and closed the laptop. The videos had confirmed the accounts given him by the employees at the rehab center. He pondered his choices. His conviction that Clark had been murdered was unshaken, yet everything pointed to suicide. But other parts of the mystery didn't add up to suicide. Clark would had taken his meds and then killed himself. That didn't make sense. He'd been able to unscrew the overhead florescent tubes even though he couldn't walk. He'd hung the chair on the door even though no one would think to come in until after he was dead.

This was no suicide.

The detective considered his list of possible suspects. If someone had engineered the murder, there would have to be a motive, and they would have had to been able to tamper with the videos. Another patient might have done it. Any businessman with Clark's influence would have acquired a substantial enemies list. Pfalzgraf's men had been unable to identify a patient who had the motive or the facility to perpetuate such a crime.

The only possible motive Pfalzgraf could come up with for the employees was that Clark might close the rehab center and they'd lose their jobs.

After some consideration, Pfalzgraf ruled Nurse Pullen out. If Pullen wanted to kill Clark, he could have done it with medications. An old guy expiring in a nursing home following a stroke wouldn't raise alarms. There wouldn't even be an autopsy. He wouldn't have needed to go to all the trouble to fabricate a locked-door suicide.

Dempsey, however, had access to the computer system, and he'd admitted that Clark's nephew had shown him how to get inside the code. But Pullen and Walton would have had to have been in on it. Their account of the events put Dempsey outside the locked door when the faked suicide went down.

The lab tech had e-mailed the edited videos to Pfalzgraf's laptop. He had asked for clips showing arrivals and departures and whatever there was at Clark's room before, during, and after the shooting. He studied the frames carefully, one by one, using the computer to step though the sequences. Then he called the lab.

"Jerry," he said, "I need you to re-examine those videos looking for something specific. Here's what I want to know..."

Just as he'd eliminated Pullen from the suspect list, Pfalzgraf eliminated Walton after a brief interview. Either the guy was a great actor or he was just too dumb to have engineered such an elaborate hoax. A check of his personnel files showed an I.Q. of about sixty-five, and he'd been employed there a long time. He couldn't have faked being that dumb for that long.

That left Dempsey among the suspect employees. The main problem was that for Dempsey to have done it, he'd have needed Pullen and Walton to back him up. They'd have to know something that was being held back, which was, how could Dempsey have gotten in that room, shot Clark, and come out without a trace of it being captured on the videos. Given that, he eliminated Dempsey, knowing he could always move him to the top of the list if nothing else panned out.

Then his phone rang. Jerry, the lab technician, had news. The videos had been tampered with just as Pfalzgraf had suspected. He called the desk sergeant and asked to have some uniforms dispatched to pick up the only suspect Pfalzgraf had who hadn't been eliminated.

Randall Clark sat across from Detective Pfalzgraf in the interrogation room at police headquarters. He was thirtyish with a slim build and wore an expensive navy blue suit.

Pfalzgraf was now properly dressed according to department policy in a brown suit with a jacket and trousers that almost matched. His tie was his favorite, blemished at the edge by a tiny blotch of egg yolk from some long ago breakfast. He still wore running shoes, but this time with white socks.

A laptop on the table sat open facing him. He kept a notepad and pencil nearby.

A uniform stuck his head in. "Detective Pfalzgraf, the lieutenant's on the phone."

Pfalzgraf stepped out to take the call.

"Detective," the lieutenant said, "I'm told you have Randall Clark in an interrogation room."

"Yes sir?"

"Is he a suspect in his uncle's death?"

"Not officially. I'm just interviewing him. He's a person of interest."

'Don't botch this one, Detective Pfalzgraf. You're already on thin ice. With the death of his uncle that kid is now the most powerful man in town. He could make life miserable for us."

"Yes, sir."

"And if my life is miserable, guess how yours is going to be."

"Yes, sir."

"Tread carefully, Detective, but close this case." He hung up.

Pfalzgraf stared at the phone, placed it gently in its cradle, and returned to the interrogation room. He sat and faced Randall Clark.

"Mr. Clark, you work at your uncle's company?"

"Yes. I'm system administrator and chief programmer."

Pfalzgraf scribbled notes as they talked. "Will you share in the estate?"

"I'm sole heir," Randall said.

Pfalzgraf tapped his pencil on the notepad and looked at Clark. "So the company will be yours? You get everything, lock, stock, and barrel?"

"Yes."

Pfalzgraf leaned forward, fixed his stare on Randall and said, "Quite a promotion. From techie to CEO. Sounds like a motive to me."

Randall drew back and glared at the detective. "Motive? It was suicide."

"So we were supposed to think. I'll need your cell phone, please." Pfalzgraf held out his hand.

Randall shifted his weight in the chair. "What's this all about?"

"Just give me the phone." Pfalzgraf tapped on the tabletop with the eraser end of his pencil. "Put it there. I'll explain in a minute."

"Don't you need a warrant?"

"I have one." The detective passed a document over to Randall. "It gives me access to your office, your home, and your phone. We'll start with the phone."

Randall read the warrant and then placed the phone on the table. Pfalzgraf carefully slid it into an evidence envelope, sealed it, and wrote on the label. Then he made a call on his own phone. A couple minutes later a young man in a white smock stuck his head in. Pfalzgraf handed him the envelope and said, "Jerry, process it right away and get back to me." He turned to Randall. "I'm going to lay out what we have. Are you willing to answer questions?"

Randall shifted in his chair again, took out a handkerchief and mopped his brow. "I think maybe I need my lawyer in here."

"Maybe, maybe not. Say the word, and I'll clam up, and you can call him. I have to read you your rights now."

Randall folded his arms and pressed back in his chair. He tightened his lips as if to remind himself not to respond. Pfalzgraf recited the Miranda warning, and Randall nodded to indicate that he understood his rights.

Pfalzgraf pulled his chair up to the laptop. “First I want you to watch some video.”

He rotated the laptop toward Randall and clicked the play button. He made no comment as they watched Randall check in at the front desk wearing a black outfit. Then the video switched to outside of Clark’s room. Nothing happened.

Randall frowned. Pfalzgraf stopped the video. “You came to see your uncle. But you didn’t go in. Hmm. This next clip is from later.”

He started the video again on which Nurse Pullen went into the room and then came out.

“Notice that he turns the light on when he goes in and turns it off when he comes out.”

For about ten minutes nothing happens and then Nurse Pullen returned.

“Se his reaction?” the detective said. “That’s when he heard the gunshot.” A few moments pass. “And here come the guard and the maintenance guy.” They watched in silence as Walton popped the hinge pins and the three men went in the room. Nothing happened for a while. Then Pfalzgraf spoke. “Here’s where they come out. We can stop watching here. We have all we need. Did you catch it?”

“Catch what?” Randall asked.

“The parts where you slipped in and out of the room.”

Randall sat forward. “What? I didn’t see anything like that.”

“No, you didn’t because that’s when the video stopped recording and started playing a repeat of the same frame of the empty hallway for a while.”

Randall squirmed in his chair. “What are you talking about? Why do you think that?”

“Because, Randall, when the three men went into the room, they used a flashlight. But in the video, the room inside stays dark for about a half minute. Not even a glimmer of the flashlight. When I got suspicious, I had our lab boys analyze that sequence. Every frame is identical down to the last pixel except for the time stamp. That would be impossible, wouldn’t you say? “

Randall didn’t answer.

"Something would have changed," Pfalzgraf said. "A fly buzzing by, a light flickering, something. That's how I knew you'd rigged the video."

"This is really stupid," Randall said, "There's nothing there that implicates me."

"See, that was your mistake. You figured it would automatically be ruled a suicide and that we'd forget about it. But you made too many mistakes that turn up when you don't assume suicide."

"Like what?"

A knock came on the door of the interrogation room. The door opened, and Jerry handed Pfalzgraf a sheet of paper. Pfalzgraf sat for a moment and scanned the document, pursing his lips from time to time and nodding. Then he said, "Your cell phone has a copy of the security system's remote controller app."

"We installed the system. Why wouldn't I have the controller app?"

"Modified? Your copy doesn't match the original according to our tech. Only a computer hacker could do that."

"So what? I was fiddling with it to see how we could improve it."

"Then there's your fingerprints on the fluorescent tube."

"How do you know they're my prints? I haven't given anybody my prints."

"Yes, you have. We lifted them off your telephone just now."

"Geez, what else?"

"Oh, there's plenty. Your uncle's prints were on the gun, but they were from the paralyzed hand. How dumb was that? And the wound was in the wrong side of his head. And there was no GSR on his head or hand, which means somebody shot him from a ways back. It just keeps piling up, Randall. You're getting in deeper and deeper."

Randall hung his head.

Pfalzgraf continued. "How did your prints get on the gun's cartridges? How come killers never think about fingerprints on the rounds? Dumber and dumber."

Randall leaned his head back and stared at the ceiling.

"So, Randall, here's how it plays out. You hacked the security system to freeze and unfreeze recording with commands from your cell phone. During that time, the system duplicates the most recent frame of video."

Pfalzgraf waited, but Randall didn't respond.

"When you got to your uncle's floor, I'm guessing you hid in a dark corner in the hallway and waited for the nurse to leave. Then you froze the video, went in his room, and unfroze the video. You were in, but there's no video record of you even being there. So far, so good."

Randall didn't respond so Pfalzgraf went on. "You disabled the lights, rigged the chair to the door, shot your uncle, and pressed his hand to the gun for his prints. The paralyzed hand, by the way."

The pained look on Randall's face told Pfalzgraf that he was hitting close to home. He continued. "I'm thinking that you waited until you heard the cart before shooting your uncle. You needed somebody to break in so you could sneak out and leave what had been a locked door to make it look like suicide."

"Man, I'm not believing this."

"Wait. It gets better. When the three guys broke in, you froze the video and hid in the dark, and while they were reacting to having found your uncle dead, you slipped out. They never saw you, which was your plan, and that's why you dressed in black and disabled the lights. When you were clear of the hallway, you unfroze the video and went out the back way. And that's about it."

"Boy, that's a stretch," Randall said. "You think you can get anyone to go for that wild tale?"

"Well, a judge went for it enough to issue the warrant. I think the D.A. will, too, and probably a jury. Now you have two choices." Pfalzgraf slid a yellow writing tablet and a pen across the table. "You can write it all down, sign it, and we'll charge you, which takes the death penalty off the table. Or you can wait for your lawyer, and he can try to cut you a better deal. If he can. Up to you."

Randall slumped in the chair and stared at the floor. Then he picked up the pen, pulled the tablet in front of him, and studied the blank yellow page. Pfalzgraf left the room to let him decide.

The Best Piano Player in Town

Charlie Bentworth ferociously slammed the keyboard cover of the grand piano. Damn Chopin! He had the infuriating habit of putting his masterworks just out of Charlie's reach. After six hours of intensive practice, Charlie still could not execute the four-measure passage that ended the C# minor part and introduced the Db major part of the Fantaisie-Impromptu. He could play the entire piece without missing a note except for that stupid run and the last page, which was eighteen measures of the same excruciating fingering. Three-two-five-one, three-two-five-one against octaves with the left hand. Human hands were not built for such impossible dexterity. Why couldn't Chopin have left that part out? Why did those guys always suck a pianist into thinking he might master a piece, only to sneak one little impossible passage into the work? Charlie's limited skill with the classics was the source of all his unhappiness. A failed marriage and an only son who never wrote or called should have gotten the best of him, and would have gotten the best of many of his contemporaries, but Charlie rolled with those setbacks just as he did with most of the other hurdles life threw into his path. Take it in stride, keep on rolling. Everything took a back seat to his number one ambition, to become a great classical pianist, and Charlie was willing to do anything to reach that goal. His failures as a husband and parent were of secondary importance to their cause, his obsessive dedication to his unreachable goal. More than once he had wanted to take his son's old baseball bat out of the hall closet and beat the piano into splinters. Those brief moments of temper were always softened, though, when he stepped back, looked at the instrument, and loved it.

Unfortunately, Charlie lacked talent. He was a fair cocktail pianist, good enough to make a living at the piano bars in the small beach resort community where he lived. But his talent ended where his ambition picked up. For twenty years Charlie had taken a lesson every week from Dr. Latta, the elderly teacher who lived a few blocks away. Twenty years of lessons on Saturday, two hours of practice every day, four to six hours on Sundays, Mondays off. He could play every major and minor scale flawlessly, both hands. He could play trills, exercises, and the simpler compositions of the masters, although without much inspiration, and he could play parts of most well-known advanced piano compositions. But every one of them had at least one passage that he could not play.

Yesterday Dr. Latta had announced that there would be no more lessons for Charlie. The Maestro was retiring from teaching all but the youngest, most promising students. Charlie hated the little snots who occupied the half-hour sessions after his own on Saturday. They came and they went, but whichever moppet was there would flop down at Dr. Latta's Steinway console and pound out a perfect recital of the current lesson. Without fail it was a piece that Charlie never finished.

Now the lessons were over. Dr. Latta spent yesterday's session counseling Charlie to ease up on himself, to accept his limitations and draw pleasure from his abilities no matter what their extent. But Charlie found no satisfaction in the applause he drew from a throwaway rendition of "New York, New York," "Feelings," or "As Time Goes By" at the Lamp Post Lounge. It would be a Rachmaninoff concerto at Carnegie Hall or nothing. He resented Dr. Latta's opinion of him. Without saying so, the Maestro had lumped Charlie in with the several matronly, blue-haired dilettantes that the professor was similarly dismissing as students.

Charlie left the piano and went out on his balcony. Gazing across the small lake behind his apartment complex, he thought about the odd thing that had happened on his way home from his final lesson. Charlie always stopped at the mall for a cup of coffee and to read the paper. The newsstand had recently added one of those fortune-telling machines with a TV screen and a typewriter-like keyboard, similar to a desktop computer. Charlie had not given it much notice, but yesterday, as he stood in line waiting to pay for his newspaper, the machine caught his attention. The screen was flashing a message and beeping softly. The message said, "Make a wish, Charlie." No one else seemed to notice it. He wondered what coincidence made the machine use his name. Perhaps the last player was named Charlie, too, and had not completed the game.

Without giving it much thought, Charlie walked over to the machine and typed on its keyboard, "I want to be the best pianist in Cordoba Beach."

The machine whirred and buzzed for a moment and flashed this message on the screen, "Your wish shall be granted." Then the screen went dark, waiting for the next player to drop a quarter into the slot. Charlie laughed and returned to the newsstand counter. Now, sitting on his balcony the following evening, he wondered about the machine's game and whether he had any hope of ever getting his wish.

It was Sunday afternoon. Charlie had Sunday nights off at the Lamp Post. The TV had little to offer on a Sunday. Charlie sat through an old movie and waited for the news at six. There was a local item about Dr. Latta's young students receiving a grant to perform at a Moscow piano competition. They'd be leaving in a few days and would be gone for three weeks. Great, thought Charlie. It would be good to get rid of the little brats for a while. Maybe this program was why the Maestro had trimmed his practice to only the youngest and best. Maybe Charlie could get back into lessons when the tour was over. Dr. Latta was not going on the tour himself because of his age and fragile health. Charlie thought maybe he'd wait and call the professor after the kids were gone.

Rather than hanging around the apartment, Charlie decided to go down to the Lagoon Lounge where Joe Pastorini played. Joe was a wonderful pianist who had a job just like Charlie's. The difference was that Joe could play. His renditions of the tunes that the resort crowd liked to hear were far better than Charlie's. Joe knew chord substitutions and voicings that amazed Charlie. His technique was beyond belief. He would insinuate dazzling keyboard runs into every song using either hand. He knew that Charlie was impressed, and he would turn on the razzle-dazzle whenever Charlie came in. If the crowd was small, Joe would entertain Charlie by playing the classical pieces that Charlie could not play. Joe was not showing off or trying to humiliate Charlie. He loved the music and loved to share his talent and was grateful to have such an appreciative audience.

The Lagoon was only a half mile from Charlie's apartment, so he usually walked. When he got to the entrance, he noticed that the sign with Joe's name and picture was gone. Inside, no one was at the piano, and the overhead spotlight that usually shone on Joe's bald head was dark. Charlie went up to the bar.

"Where's Joe?" he asked the bartender.

The bartender hestitated, then said, "You didn't hear? He had an accident on his mo-ped yesterday. Got hit by a car. Broke his arm in three places. Had a concussion, too."

"My God! Where is he?"

"The hospital. He'll be there a couple of days. His wife called today. We'll be looking for a new piano player, I guess. Want the job?"

Charlie shook his head and left the lounge. He walked back to his apartment in a daze. Joe's arm broken. How bad? Would he ever play again? Charlie went up the stairs and went inside. He called Joe's wife. She was just home from visiting Joe, and she was crying. Joe wouldn't be working for a while. She was worried about money. They had no insurance, and the car that hit Joe didn't stop. Charlie promised to help her in any way he could and hung up. What a tragedy, he thought. He resolved to visit Joe as often as he could. What an irony, as well. Now, with Joe out of commission, Charlie was the best piano player in the local lounge circuit. They'd even offered him Joe's job. What a stupid thought. As if that video game was somehow responsible.

The next day Charlie went back to the mall to get a card and maybe a plant to take to Joe. He stopped by the newsstand for a couple of magazines that Joe would like. Standing in line he tried to ignore the electronic fortune teller. No use, it compelled him to look. The screen had this message, "You're one step closer to your wish, Charlie." He was stunned. What did it mean? He raced over to the machine and typed the one word, "What?" The machine quietly went dark.

At the hospital, Joe was glad to see him. They talked about a lot of things, but Charlie did not mention the machine or his wish. The next day would be the departure of Dr. Latta's students. The thought made Charlie nervous. With those kids out of town, there would be even fewer pianists better than him, and it bothered him.

On Tuesday, Charlie watched the local news coverage when Dr. Latta's students boarded the plane for the trip to Moscow. The newscaster explained the gloom that hung over the children on what should have been a happy occasion. The evening before, Dr. Latta had passed away in his sleep, never to know the outcome of the competition for which he had prepared his students for so long. Charlie could barely believe it. Although his better judgment said otherwise, he was now certain that the video game's fortune teller had something to do with all this. He didn't know how, but there were just too many coincidences. There must be something he could do to stop whatever was happening.

Calming down, he decided to make a list of all the pianists in town who were better than him. That wouldn't be hard, he thought, just list all the pianists. But his list was shorter than he thought. It was a small town.

There were only two such pianists that he knew about, the music teacher at the high school, and the organist at the Methodist church. Charlie had heard the organist, Henry Butterfield, play piano when the choir performed gospel music on the local television station. He was very good as was the high school teacher. And he'd heard Mrs. Penrose trying out pianos in the music store in the mall.

How could Charlie warn them, how could he get them to leave town before it was too late?

"Mrs. Penrose, I'm Charlie Bentworth, one of Dr. Latta's students. I called to see if you had heard about Dr. Latta's passing." Charlie used the professor's death as a reason to call the high school teacher. He wasn't sure how he was going to explain the real reason for his call. Perhaps she'd provide an opening. She'd probably think he was a nut.

"Yes, Mr. Bentworth, what a sad loss. But he had been sick for a while, and he was rather advanced in years."

"And to happen just when the children were going to Moscow. Were any of them your students at the high school?"

"Just one, but two more will be advancing next year. I must say it speaks well of Dr. Latta's teaching ability to know that there are so many talented students right here in our little town. He could probably have taught anyone to play well."

That last remark stung. “Yes, well I suppose you’ll be taking over some of his students now that he is gone.”

“Well, no, not really. I have my own little tragedy to cope with. Arthritis. The doctor diagnosed it just yesterday, as a matter of fact. I won’t be playing the piano any more, I’m sorry to say.”

Three down, one to go. This is getting out of hand.

“I’m certainly sorry to hear that,” Charlie said, and he meant it. “It’s been good to talk to you, Mrs. Penrose. Now I’d better ring off. I want to call Henry Butterfield just in case he hasn’t heard.”

“Don’t bother,” she snapped back. “You won’t find him anywhere to be found.”

“How’s that?” Charlie was afraid to hear the explanation.

“Mr. Butterfield tried to leave town this morning along with the choir director’s wife and the better part of the new church organ fund taken right out of the bank. Mr. Butterfield was signatory, you know.”

“No, I didn’t. They must have trusted him, though.”

“They did. The pastor is extremely upset not to mention my husband, who is the church board’s finance officer. That’s how I happened to know before anyone else. The worse part is that our dear choir director took his hunting shotgun and shot Mr. Butterfield dead and is in jail at this very moment. Scandalous and tragic. Not that I care to gossip, mind you, but I just thought I’d save you the trouble of a call.”

That put the cap on it. Those kids would be coming home soon, most of them better players than Charlie. An airplane crash would complete the fortune teller’s fulfillment. Charlie said goodbye, ran to the closet to get one item, and sprinted down the stairs and into the parking lot to his car to drive to the mall.

The video fortune teller was sitting in its corner, glowing and humming. As he walked up to it, the screen flashed a message. “Done. Your wish has been granted, Charlie.” Charlie was livid. He wanted to scream at the machine, to grab it by the shoulders and shake it apart. But it didn’t have any shoulders. And yelling wouldn’t work. Trembling, he did what he knew to do, he typed, “What about when the students come home from Moscow and Joe’s arm heals and Mrs. Penrose’s arthritis gets better? Are you going to kill them too?” The machine dimmed and appeared to be regarding his question. Then it said, “A permanent wish, Charlie? Reconsidering given new information.”

Charlie was ready. He swung the baseball bat in a wide arc. It struck the side of the video monitor with full force, shattering the screen and causing sparks and smoke to spill out of the cabinet. The next blow came from directly overhead, landing squarely on the machine’s keyboard. Little keycaps and springs went flying everywhere. The final strike was at the side of the square box where the machine was mounted. The box bent and collapsed and its ruined circuit boards came poking out where the sides separated from the force of Charlie’s blow.

The newsstand attendant was yelling at Charlie to stop. The other customers were staring in disbelief. Some of them had dropped their parcels as they watched the spectacle in horror. Several passersby stopped to gawk in. Seeing that the machine was now completely destroyed, Charlie lowered the bat, walked up to the counter, and, still breathing heavily, pulled a card from his wallet. It said Charlie Bentworth, Pianist, and had his phone number on it. He gave the card to the attendant and gasped, “Tell whoever owns that piece of junk to call me. I’ll pay for it.” Then he stormed out, leaving everyone there still not believing what they had just seen.

As he drove home, Charlie wondered what the machine would cost him. Maybe he’d be sharing a cell with the Methodist choir director. He never got that call, however, and never again saw another machine like it. But at home that afternoon, for what had to be at least the five thousandth time, Charlie played Chopin’s Fantaisie-Impromptu and, with a new feeling of accomplishment, once again played it wrong.

The Stache

The black tarmac was hard under Eddie's feet. The parking lot was the warmest ground surface to be found on this cold January morning, and the seagulls and grackles huddled on it, being chased by the cars of the NASA workers as they slowly filled the lot. Eddie pulled his windbreaker tightly around him and made the short hike across the lot to the rear entrance of the Kennedy Space Center Headquarters building. Traffic had been heavy this morning because of the tourists who crowd into town for every Shuttle launch. They line the causeway and the road that leads to Port Canaveral and Cape Canaveral Air Force Station. They picnic and party and visit, enjoying the vacation atmosphere and the thrill of sharing a Shuttle launch, being there to see it live. No one that day could foresee the spectacle of horror that awaited them. Eddie was a few minutes late to work because of them. He went into the cafeteria through the rear entrance to get breakfast, which he carried out today. He was late for the installation of the new version of the program he was working on. The elevator took him to the second floor where his project had its offices. He wolfed down the breakfast while his desktop computer compiled and linked a production version of the program to install in the test site, an office of engineers and word processor operators down the hall. The computer run and his breakfast were finished at about the same time. He copied the program to a diskette and took it to the site where Pearl was waiting.

Pearl always had a big grin for Eddie. She liked him because he made her laugh with his jokes, and he was always ready to make little changes to the software in response to her suggestions. A tall, full-bodied brunette with a pronounced Georgia accent, Pearl was in charge of the users' side of the tests, and she was the lead operator of the program as well.

Eddie loaded the new program in and ran a test. Pearl watched over his shoulder while he stepped through the menus and ran some of the new options. The new version was working okay, although it was sluggish. Eddie frowned and shook his head. The NASA guys couldn't leave anything alone. They kept adding useless features to what had been an efficient and effective program. He had written the first version for them two years ago, and it had been a hit. The NASA guy who was in charge of the project got a lot of brownie points for its success, so now they couldn't leave it alone. Everybody wants to ride a winner. The only way to keep the ride going was to keep making improvements, needed or not. Everybody wants a piece of a hit. You can build a career on having something to do with something that works well. Government middle managers are always more interested in their careers than their jobs, he thought. Pearl's attitude was that it kept her and Eddie employed by the contractor that supported the engineers. Eddie would rather be doing something meaningful.

He heard the distant crackle of the speakers in the hall. Every hallway had one. They broadcast the countdowns so the employees could keep up with the launches. Mission Control was talking from Houston, but Eddie couldn't tell what they were saying. He was too involved in finishing the installation.

Pearl said, "They're almost ready to launch the Shuttle. Are you going to watch?"

"Yeah, I guess so. I haven't missed one yet. You coming?"

"No, I've got to finish up here."

Eddie shut down the computer and walked down the long corridor past his inside office to the north side of the building. The NASA executives with window offices generously let the contractors—who never got window offices—come in to watch a launch. It was old hat by now. Most people just listened to the speakers without getting up. Eddie always watched.

Eddie stood next to an old guy who always watched, too. They had watched Saturn launches together from the roof of the Manned Spacecraft Operations Building—now called Operations and Control—in the 60s.

The old guy hadn't been so old back then. Neither had Eddie. The Space Coast had been an exciting place, staffed by young engineers and support people. The social scene on a Friday after work was vibrant and interesting. There were plenty of bars with plenty of unattached—or attached but errant—young people. Eddie was married then, but he fell into the party scene often enough to know how it worked. When he returned to the area after an absense of some years, he found the same people, except that now they were older. Most of them went home after work on Friday. A lot of the watering holes had closed; others had become pool halls or redneck hangouts. Only a few of the original live spots were left, and some of them catered to their same old clientelle, except that the once-youthful party animals were now just faded bar flies, hanging on to a past that would not return. Eddie still went to the Mousetrap, but it wasn't the same.

"Cold today," the old guy said. "Even for January. It's in the low twenties, I think. Some of my plants got killed in the frost last night."

It was indeed cold for January in Florida. Eddie lived on his sailboat and had used several extra blankets last night. He knew a little bit about aviation, too, from his association with a flying bartender friend, and he told the old guy, "Airplanes fly better in cold air. I wonder if the same is true for Space Shuttles." They'd never launched one this cold. He'd heard that this launch was important, no delays if possible. Reagan wanted a show stopper for his State of the Union speech. No one knew how much of a one he was going to get.

The countdown was in the final minute. The Mission Control guy was stepping down the sequence with detached efficiency. Eddie could hear him clearly now. This was nothing like the first shuttle launch in '81 with news people every where and commentators stupidly trying to make news when things got slow by speculating on the air about what would happen if the tiles fell off. Now, almost five years later, Space Shuttle launches were routine as far as the rest of the world was concerned. There was still plenty of interest, but the suspense wasn't there.

Eddie's job was not directly associated with launches or flight hardware. He'd pledged to himself nineteen years before never to get that close to the actual mission again. He worked on support systems, instead.

Supply, spare parts, engineering document management, CAD/CAM, everything on the periphery, nothing connected to the bird. But he still felt a sense of belonging and pride, and he always watched.

As the countdown reached the last few seconds, they announced the clearance for main engine ignition. The engines lit up on cue, the vehicle vibrated and strained to lift off, and then the boosters kicked in. As usual, the flame was almost too bright to look at. Challenger left the pad slowly in its great white cloud of smoke and flame, rose, delicately performed the routine roll manuever, and headed toward its destiny with history. Just another routine shuttle launch, the 25th one. A neglectful press and population would soon have their attention drawn abruptly away from whatever else they were doing.

Now, at about 40 degrees off the horizon, just as the rumble reached the spectators, something was different, something was very wrong. The people at the windows watched numbly while the usual flawless and brilliant spectacle violated routine. There was the expected drift-changed, wandering contrail from the launch pad to where the shuttle should be, but now, instead of terminating at the tail of the tiny spark that should be the vehicle, it went into this huge ball of smoke. The ball glowed at its center, a holocaust. Now there were two new and aimless contrails with fiery tips streaking out of the top of the ball like Roman candles going in different directions. Apparently, the boosters were flying on their own, separated from the craft well before they were supposed to. Eddie couldn't remember seeing the ball form or the boosters first coming out of it. It was as if he had looked away. But he never looked away, not once.

No one in the room said anything. No one moved. Everyone expected to see the orbiter come gliding out of that ball of fire and smoke to return on deadstick to the landing site. A manned launch had never aborted after liftoff, and no one there knew what one should look like. They just assumed that they were watching an orderly abort, not the horror that was happening and, later, obvious in retrospect. After a long silence, Mission Control said simply, hollowly, "We have a major malfunction."

A gradual, dull understanding of what they were seeing washed over the few in that room and over the tens of thousands of other spectators around the agency, around the world.

Now the ball of smoke was spreading, and burning debris came falling from inside it to the ocean thousands of feet below. They could not see the particles of debris; they could see only the trails of smoke they left. There were hundreds of those trails. The burning pieces of disintegrated hardware rained down for a long time, each one cooling as it reached the ocean. Later, Eddie remembered with wonder the evening launch he'd watched from his sailboat in the ocean just about where those pieces were falling now. But now, all he thought about were the seven people, one of them a school teacher, sent by the politicians to stir public interest in the program, their deadly plummet to earth defined by one of those traces of smoke, which one no one knew.

You don't know how to feel. No experience prepares you for one like this. There is the need to say something out loud to make it easier, but no knowledge of what to say. There is a call from inside to think or feel something other than what you are knowing now, to lessen the pain, shift the load. The question, "why?" echos in your mind. Every one around you asks themselves the same question. You don't hear it but you know. They all know. Their individual memories of lives occasioned by other random and meaningless losses silently haunt and remind each solitary observer that they will never know the answer.

One by one, people came out of the offices into the halls. The ones who did not bother to watch came, too, from the inner parts of the building. They wanted to get closer to the hallway speakers to hear what happened, and they wanted to be with each other, not to discuss or revisit it, but to be with others who shared what they had seen. That could not have just happpened. We are still alive. This is inconsistent. No one spoke. They just looked at one another, waiting, listening, their eyes asking desperately to be told somehow that it would not be as they knew it must. Some of them wept silently. They had just seen seven people blown to Kingdom Come, and they felt without knowing that they were changed forever for having seen it. The picture of catastrophe raining from a billow of fire and smoke, turning finally into a wisp and lingering in the Eastern sky for most of the morning, would stay with them, burned into their memories, to be painfully refreshed for months afterward every time they looked at a newspaper or a magazine or turned on the news.

One thing Eddie was sure of, when the shock subsided and he sat at his desk, was that things would be different at work for a while. He remembered with a dull ache another day nineteen years before when the Apollo fire brought the space program to a temporary halt. It was January then, too

The next six months at Kennedy Space Center had been pure hell. Every movement made by a person of consequence was calculated to divert the potential for blame elsewhere. It would happen again this time.

The stress of the Apollo fire's aftermath had weakened Eddie's marriage, and his wife had left him. Now he lived on his sailboat. The Florida climate was suited for that way of life, and there was work for him here. He took a job on a contract as far away from the flight hardware as possible, never wanting to repeat the inquisition of 1967. Now it would happen all over again.

Eddie looked around the office, picked up the few items that were his, and left the building, not looking back. He drove off the center, through the Air Force station, and stopped at the guard post on the way out to hand his picture badge to a surprised guard. He'd take care of the formalities of a resignation later. He drove off the base and to the marina at the port where he lived on his boat, changed into shorts and a T-shirt, and drove south to Cocoa Beach to Ramon's where Mickey worked as a bartender.

Mickey had been Eddie's friend since Eddie had returned. Once the proprietor of a bar where Eddie hung out, Mickey had lost the place after he was arrested on suspicion of dealing drugs from the bar. The judge dropped the charges for lack of evidence or an improper search or something, and Eddie had never asked Mickey whether there was anything to the charges. The costs of his defense had wiped Mickey out, however, and now he worked for someone else.

Mickey and Eddie used to fly together. Before his trouble, Mickey had owned a Cessna 210, and they spent many weekends cruising the

Bahamas or going to the Keys. Now they made shorter trips in Eddie's boat. Mickey sure knew his way around the islands, and Eddie had often wondered how Mickey had gotten that experience and how far south it extended. Now he intended to find out.

Eddie had always stayed mostly within the law. He didn't mess with funny substances, but he didn't judge those who did. There was always the nagging notion that there was money to be made from those people, but Eddie had always respected the rules of the establishment and didn't really want to risk his career or future by breaking them. Now the establishment as he knew it had just taken its terminal plunge. There was nothing left to hold him to his faltering convictions. There was nothing left to hold his interest, either. Maybe some adventure would revitalize his life. Besides, he just couldn't give a damn about consequences anymore. Seven other straight arrows had played by the rules to make it as astronauts, and now they were at the bottom of the ocean, the victims of ambitious politicians and bureaucrats who couldn't postpone a trendy mission that the president could brag about.

Eddie talked and Mickey listened. How often, Eddie wondered, had they sailed from the Atlantic Ocean into Port Canaveral without attracting attention? Any time of day or night. Airplanes were tracked on radar and were supposed to go through customs, but any small boat that came in without clearing customs was assumed to be returning from a recreational ocean sail. Mickey agreed, wondering where this was going. Therefore, Eddie continued, a boat with a load of contrabandcould enter without notice. Mickey agreed, beginning to understand and wondering at this apparent change in his usually conservative buddy. Eddie outlined a plan, one that would take an investment of money, both of them as principal participants, and the right contacts if they could find them. That's where Mickey offered what Eddie hoped he could. Mickey had the contacts, someone who would set up the source, bankroll the operation, and take delivery of the product.

"That's the hitch," Eddie said. "There won't be any product for several years. We'll bring the stuff in, put the boat in drydock, and leave it there until we're ready to retire. Then, we'll dispose of the product."

"Why wait?" asked Mickey.

"So we don't take any chances. If anybody's watching, they'll have to watch that boat for years. I'm leaving the area. The boat stays here in drydock until I'm ready to cash in the cargo, which will be carefully tucked away in the hull. By then, who'll pay any attention when I pull it out of the yard?"

"Nobody'll bankroll that kind of operation. They'll want immediate delivery."

"Then we'll have to do it ourselves. There's two things we need if you can set up the source. One is a seaplane with good range, and the other is the money to buy the product."

"The seaplane's no problem. I have a buddy who's got one and I can borrow it. For a decent buy, though, we'll need about fifty grand."

"OK, I'll mortgage the boat, sell my car, and cash in my retirement. How much do we figure to make?"

"Who knows in several years? Maybe ten times our investment. Maybe more. We could schedule our sale to coincide with when product is scarce and get a better price."

"Are you in?"

"I'm in."

It took several months to get the money together. During that time, Eddie went north to get a job in the Washington, DC area. He used his experience to land a spot with one of the "beltway bandits," the government contractors who flourished around the capitol beltway. The abrupt departure from the KSC contractor presented a problem, but Eddie had security clearances and valuable skills. They outweighed his presumed lapse of responsibility, which he blamed on the emotional hit the Challenger accident had occasioned.

With a job, he could negotiate a loan against the boat. It took as long to collect his vested interest in his retirement fund from his former employer. Soon he had the money they needed.

Mickey used his contacts to establish a source in South America. Eddie soon learned that Mickey knew a lot more about the procedures than he had let on. Mickey would handle the buy and the pickup and would deliver the cargo to the boat. Eddie had to get the boat to the transfer location.

They had studied the nautical charts for a long time to select a likely location. The site had to be remote and hidden, perhaps a cove that Eddie could hide in and where Mickey could land safely in the ocean. They chose the seaplane rather than a land airplane because they wanted the freedom to change plans at any time, and they did not want to be close to other people, a guarantee they could not make if a runway was needed. They chose a quiet cove on the north side of an uninhabited island. On a warm Sunday in May, Eddie, on leave from his new job, set sail alone. Mickey waited a couple of days and took off in the borrowed seaplane for the pickup point in South America. He took with him the cash and enough personal documentation to clear customs when he returned to the mainland.

Eddie's sail was without event. He located the cove, entered, and weighed anchor. According to their plan, he went ashore at night to scout the small island for inhabitants. No one was there. Everything was perfect. He returned to the boat and settled in to wait the night for Mickey.

The next morning he turned on the Citizen's Band radio, tuned in channel 10, and listened. At about 10:30 he heard the sound he wanted to hear. Someone far away was keying a microphone on that channel. He waited for the pause they'd agreed to and keyed twice in return. Mickey's acknowledging key sequence came back. That was their code. Everything was on target. The illegal high-powered CB radios had done their job. No one hearing the noise on the frequency would think anything about it.

Eddie put on his bathing suit, got his tools together, and slipped over the side. Mickey was on his way, and there was little time to waste. He slowly, meticulously measured and cut a large rectangular hole, about three feet by five feet, in the side of the hull, just above the water line. He put the fiberglass cut-out up onto the deck. Then he swam around and made a similar aperture in the other side. He pulled himself out of the water, climbed topside, and had lunch. The job had taken only an hour and a half. He laid out the tools for the rest of the job and waited.

The seaplane's drone was distant but clear. Eddie waited and watched until he could see the speck on the horizon. It grew larger and then took the shape of the seaplane. Mickey had dropped down to about

100 feet above the sea and was coming in fast and straight, expertly, as if he had done this before. He slowed as he neared the cove. Flying a perfect arc around the tree-lined shore, Mickey pulled the throttle back and set the plane down in the blue water. The water slowed him, he turned and taxied up next to the boat.

Eddie was on deck just above where the hole gaped from the starboard side of the hull. Mickey climbed out onto the seaplane's struts, stepped onto one of the pontoons, and threw two lines to Eddie, who tied the plane to the boat's starboard stanchions. Mickey began unloading and throwing white brick-shaped packages to Eddie. They were wrapped in a heavy vinyl cellophane-like wrap and secured with duct tape. Eddie stuffed the precious bricks into canvas bags, several to a bag. The bags had draw-string ties with the ends of the lines already lashed to a stanchion. When the third bag was full, Eddie switched to a second set of bags tied to a stanchion on the port side of the boat. The last brick filled the third bag, and Mickey jumped aboard. They shook hands without speaking. Mickey grabbed one of six five-gallon gasoline containers from the deck, took it aboard the seaplane, and emptied its contents into the left wing tank. He repeated the process until all the gas containers were emptied into the plane's two tanks. Next he took the battery-powered vacuum cleaner aboard the airplane and thoroughly cleaned the cargo compartment, tossing the vacuum cleaner back on the deck of the boat when he was done. Then he untied the plane from the boat, waved to Eddie, and climbed into the cockpit. Eddie pushed him off, and Mickey started the seaplane's engines, taxied out a short distance, and took off. They hadn't spoken a word during the entire exchange.

Eddie didn't watch this time. He slung both groups of stanchion-tethered canvas bags over the sides, grabbed a knife, and jumped in after the bags. He pulled himself up close to where the bags hung down next to the hole, and shoved the bags inside the hull, cutting the line after the bags were securely inside the make-shift hold. He swam under the hull and came up on the other side to repeat the process for the bags hanging down on the other side. Then he pulled himself up on deck, retrieved one of the cutouts and a fiberglass repair kit, and dropped back down into the water. Eddie carefully placed the cutout in the hole it had formed and used the repair kit to fill around the cutout, pushing the glass paste deeply into the cracks and smoothing the glass with a putty knife. He made the same repair to the other side and went aboard. It was well into the afternoon, now and all he could do was wait for morning when the glass would be dry enough to sand and paint.

The next morning, Eddie sanded the repaired seams and spray painted them with a quick-drying paint to match the hull's orginal color. When he was done, he swam away from the boat to check his work. A casual observer would not be able to tell that there had been a repair made to either side. He swam back and pulled himself aboard for the last time. All that was left was to make it back to Port Canaveral without incident. He set sail right away, planning to sail until dark and sleep a while. He planned his trip so that he would enter the port in the late afternoon when most of the day sailers and fishing trips would be returning.

Sailing into the port was the hardest part. Eddie hadn't seen another vessel during the sail back from the rendezvous location. Now he was surrounded by them. His imagination worked overtime, expecting to be hailed and boarded by Coast Guard or DEA agents at any time. He lowered the sails and motored into the port, past the cruise ships at their docks, the Navy vessels, the commercial shrimp and scallop boats, the deep sea fishing charters, the pleasure boats, finally making his way into his slip at Cape Marina. He tied up the boat, secured the hatches, changed clothes, and went ashore. He told the marina manager that he'd be away for a while and that he wanted to put the boat into drydock for an indefinite period. The manager promised to haul the boat and store it the next day.

Eddie drove to Mickey's bar. Mickey was there. They shared a drink and agreed to keep in touch at least monthly. Mickey would watch the market for a good time to sell, and Eddie would go back to work in Washington. They figured to hold out for at least five years unless a shortage drove prices up significantly. Their trust was reinforced by their need for each other. Mickey knew who and where the buyers were. Only Eddie could retrieve the stache of product.

***

Six years passed. Eddie and Mickey talked almost monthly as they had agreed. Eddie spent all his vacations in Florida staying with Mickey, who held onto his bartending job. Eddie's employment changed with the contracts in Washington, but he always had a job. Neither of them needed the revenues that waited for them, and neither of them pushed to cash in. It was August. Mickey called Eddie long distance at his job one day. Prices were up, way up. The feds had really been cracking down, and several suppliers were out of product and hurting. Mickey had shopped around and gotten a guarantee of $750,000 for the whole cargo. The only problem was that the delivery had to be made in South Miami. Mickey was worried about getting tagged driving such a load south on I-95. Eddie told him not to worry. They'd sail it down.

Two days later, Eddie was at the Cape Marina giving the manager instructions for launching his boat. He felt alive, unemployed again, having quit his job as abruptly as he had done six years earlier, only this time for a more positive purpose. He and Mickey, also unemployed now, had their retirement already planned, a life of ocean cruising and far-away places in their future. They would do it all together. First stop, a small marina just south of Homestead, Florida, between Miami and the Keys. They planned to dock the boat there for a month before making the delivery. The buyer agreed to their schedule and would not know the delivery point until they were ready. Nothing was left to chance. Eddie was sailing alone this first leg while Mickey drove down so they'd have a car for their last month as landlubbers.

He set sail on a Saturday afternoon, the boat freshly painted and stocked with supplies—food, booze, and paperback books—the usual provisions for an ocean cruise. It took three days to make it down the coast and around the tip of the Florida peninsula to the small inlet where they had a slip reserved in the tiny, unobtrusive marina. Eddie landed the boat, tied up, and went ashore to meet Mickey, who was already there. They paid the slip fees and settled in to wait out their planned cooling off period. Their plans were set. They'd make the sale, collect the cash, sell the car, and sail to the Virgin Islands to open an off-shore bank account. Then, with an almost unlimited checking account and nothing else but time, the two mariners would cruise the oceans of the world, putting in where the spirit moved them, enjoying what the far reaches of the planet had to offer.

For four days they relaxed on the beach and hung out in several of the local bars. Transients are common in south Florida, and no one paid them any notice. On the fifth day they heard the news. Hurricane Andrew was brewing in the Atlantic, heading toward the mainland. By the sixth day, the area was in preparation for the possibility of a serious landfall. On the seventh, they were sure. Andrew would touch the southern tip of the Florida peninsula by nightfall. Eddie and Mickey secured the boat as best they could and joined the evacuation, driving north on I-95, glad they hadn't sold the car yet.

They listened to the news as they drove. Andrew was moving toward land and gaining strength. It took about five hours to drive with the heavy traffic the 200 miles to Cocoa Beach where Mickey still had his small furnished apartment. He was keeping it as a home base. They camped in front of the TV and watched and listened throughout the night as the news channel followed Andrew's progress. The descriptions of the devastating effects the hurricane had on the communities in and around Homestead had a chilling effect. They wondered and worried about how the boat and its precious cargo would fare. Suppose the hull split. Anyone could see into the makeshift hold. They tried to remember if anything they had said to the marina manager or anything they left on board would lead the authorities back to them.

Andrew pounded the southern tip of Florida throughout the night and into the next day. Then it moved into the Gulf of Mexico, eventually to make its way to Louisiana and a similar destiny. In the mean time Eddie and Mickey knew they had little choice. They had to head south and see the results.

As they drove they listened to the reports of the mass destruction. They stopped worrying about themselves as they heard the plight of thousands of newly homeless residents. It was obvious that any authorities on duty that day would not be concerned with them or the boat. There would be too much confusion, too little authority. That should work to their advantage.

The further south they drove. the heavier the traffic moving north on I-95. People weren't evacuating now. They were abandoning, leaving behind whatever was left.

Past south Miami and approaching Homestead, they became more and more aware of the extent of the damage. More accurately, they became aware that the scope of destruction was simply beyond their comprehension. They left the Interstate at the exit leading to the marina. The road was barely passable. Eddie looked in all directions as Mickey threaded the small car around the obstacles in the road. There was nothing but rubble as far as he could see. Piles of debris. Where yesterday there were rows of neat, orderly homes with nicely manicured lawns on quiet, criss-crossing streets, now there was nothing that you could recognize or identify. Here and there he saw small groups of people standing, poking around in what he supposed were the ruins of what had been their homes. He felt their desperation, wondered about their future, if they had anything now, if anything could be recovered. He tried to put himself in their shoes. The lucky ones would have enough insurance to replace their homes. He pondered the hopeless feeling of a young couple, standing in this horizon-to-horizon field of destruction with an insurance check in their hands. How can you rebuild? Why should you? So you replace your house, what then? Will there be schools, stores, jobs? The whole community superstructure that supported these neighborhoods is destroyed. What value is one family's small plot of land in such a wasteland? It is going to take years to recover, thought Eddie.

Now he had to pull his attention away from the troubles of others and back to his own survival. They were approaching the entrance to the marina. His hopes faltered. The aluminum walls and roof of the small boat storage building were down, reduced to a pile of crumpled sheet metal scattered around the remains of the boats that had been stored. They pulled into what had been a parking lot and got out of the car. Two of the docks were gone. The one where Eddie had his slip was, miraculously, still there, much the worse for wear. Most of the boats were gone, destroyed by the storm. Mickey and Eddie looked down the length of the dock and saw part of a hull sticking out of the water where the slip had been. They delicately made their way down the dock, testing with each step to be sure the footing was secure, hoping with each step that the cargo had survived.

Reaching the slip, they both saw the undeniable toll taken on their plans by Hurricane Andrew. The inverted hull, sticking out of the water, was split on both sides. There was no cargo, not one package. If it didn't get bounced and blown out of the hold during the pummelling that Andrew delivered, it was surely now in the hands of some very lucky looters. Either way, Mickey and Eddie were no longer in the wholesale drug business. They turned and walked slowly off the dock and back to the car.

Santas on Patrol

Every year Ed Yates donned his red suit, white beard, and black boots and took his position in front of the department store in the mall. He rang the bell and invited shoppers to share their change with the less fortunate. He was popular among the children and their parents, and his charity always did well by his campaign. His pot usually took in a goodly sum.

But every year for the past three on Christmas Eve, the busiest day of the season and near closing time, the same low-life creep had snuck up on him, dipped into the pot, grabbed as much currency as he could, and bolted out the mall entrance.

Ed had gotten to where he could spot the robber when he came in. He was a small man, with sneaky eyes, shabby clothes, and usually in need of a shave. But he was elusive, blended into the crowds, and always waited until Ed's attention was away from the pot, talking to a child or a parent. Then the thief would make his move, and another twenty or thirty bucks or more would be gone.

This year Ed was determined to be ready. Before setting up the first day, and after he'd put on his suit, he made the rounds and visited all the other Santas at the mall. They'd all heard about the thief, of course, and were eager to do something about him. Ed invited them to a meeting in the employee's lounge.

"Why always you?" Bill Porterfield was the Santa inside the department store, and sat for children to line up and tell him what they wanted for Christmas.

Ed made an off-putting gesture. "I guess because I'm closest to the entrance. And most of you don't collect money."

"Have you tried to catch him?" John Berryman worked the center lobby and was surrounded by helper elves who passed out candy and small gifts to the children. The elves stood by without comment during this meeting called by a Santa for all the Santas.

Ed sighed. “By the time I realize what’s happened, he’s disappeared into the crowd and out the door. I can’t even get there fast enough to see him escape in the parking lot.”

“Are you bringing mall security in on this?” Andy Barone asked.

Ed laughed. “Old Murphy? He spends most of his time sleeping. By the time he got here, the crook would be ten miles away. No, we have to do this ourselves.”

“How about the police?”

“A uniform hanging around would just scare him off. No, we want to catch him red-handed.”

“And if he yells ‘mistaken identity’?”

“He’ll have this marked twenty in his hand.” Ed showed them the bill he’d prepared. “It’ll be on top folded across the rim where he can’t miss it.”

“What kind of man does that?” they all asked. “Stealing from the needy.”

Ed shook his head. “The worst kind.”

With that, he laid out his plan for the other Santas, and they agreed. They’d have their cell phones within easy reach, and Ed would text them when the time was ready.

“It’s always happened on Christmas Eve,” he told them, “Until then let’s be prepared to move on a moment’s notice.”

The first week passed with no action. Each evening Ed would broadcast an “ALL CLEAR” text message, and each time, all six Santas responded.

On Christmas Eve, an hour before closing, the mall was packed with last-minute shoppers. Ed stood next to his pot and rang his cheerful invitation, tossing out “ho, ho, hos” to the children. But he kept his eye on the crowd.

Then he saw the sneaky thief moving in with the throng, staying on the far side of the entranceway, and skulking into the mall, soon to be lost in the crowd.

When the crook was out of sight, Ed picked up his phone and texted, “HES HERE.” Certain that the crook would be watching, Ed was careful not to take his eyes off the pot. He didn't want the strike to come before his men were in place.

Gradually, the Santas began to file in, quietly taking their posts as agreed. John Berryman had brought two of his elves.

With the volunteer red-suited vigilantes in place, Ed now gave his full attention to two children standing with their mother. He intentionally turned his back on the pot.

With that, the thief struck. He darted out of the crowd, sideswiped the mother, and grabbed the twenty and whatever more he could retrieve. Then he pushed away and into the crowd and was gone.

Ed went in hot pursuit. He elbowed his way through, to find the thief standing there, his mouth agape, as four Santas hurtled toward him. Before the crook could react, the Santas were in his face leaning over him.

Two other Santas and two elves came running up from behind and stood beside Ed. The bad guy was surrounded by Santas, and he turned first one way then the other. In a desperate move he tried to push past the four red-suited jolly old men who blocked his path to freedom. An elf tripped him, and down he went. The Santas leaned over and began pummeling him with their white gloved fists while the elves kicked him with their pointy-toed green shoes. The astonished crowd pulled away from this unlikely spectacle, and the air was filled with jingle bells ringing from the costumes and the thief yelling for mercy.

A little boy clutched his mother's arm and looked up at her. "Mom, why are those Santa Clauses beating up that man?"

"I don't know, dear. Maybe he did something bad."

His eyes teared up. "Mom, tell Santa I've been good. Very good. All year."

The One-Armed Bandit

Andy Watson unstrapped his seat belt, pushed out of the seat, and pulled his backpack down from the overhead compartment above his seat. The passengers on the crowded L-1011 pushed and shoved to get their own bags and packages from overhead and under the seats and themselves into the aisle. Most of them kept up a steady stream of Spanish as they crowded toward the door. After a time the door opened and the horde moved forward. Andy wedged himself into the line and made his way off the airplane.

Puerto Rico was hot and humid. He could feel it as soon as he left the air conditioned airplane and stepped into the passageway. He followed the crowd toward the baggage claim area. Andy had no bags to collect, but the rental car counters were just past the conveyor. He stood in line for a long time while the two agents took their time with each customer. He suppressed his impatience, and in time it was his turn. He was surprised that his reservation was there. Somehow it didn't seem possible that they would manage to have it.

Much later, in a rattletrap of the smallest Susuki a person could fit into, Andy pulled onto highway PR-26 and headed west past Isla Verde toward San Juan, where the casinos are. Andy drove until he saw the tall, glittery sign that identified the Sands Hotel and Casino.

The Sands is one of the biggest and plushest hotel-casinos in San Juan. Fashioned after its namesake in Las Vegas, it has one of the best-equipped gaming rooms in the city. The Sands sits on the east end of town among a strip of fast food joints, San Juan's concession to the tastes of mainlanders who come to the island for a tropical holiday but do not want to give up familiar conveniences. Andy stopped at Wendy's for a take-out burger. Then he drove three blocks to the Sands and parked in the dark parking lot across the street. He ate his dinner sitting in the car with the door standing open. While he ate he gazed at the lights coming from inside the casino and wondered how much longer his plan would continue to work. There was no reason why it wouldn't. Andy had spent most of his spare time for the last two years working out the details. He thought he'd considered every possibility but couldn't be sure. This was his third time out.

The surf maintained its steady gentle pounding from just beyond the casino. A car alarm went off somewhere, a shrill oscillating siren. The little tree lizards called geckos chirped their occasional shrill cat-like squeak. The sounds of San Juan were familiar to him from a long time ago.

A small island dog timidly approached Andy hoping for a handout. Every parking lot in San Juan has one or two of these strays. They live in the alleys and under the parked cars, begging handouts from tourists. Andy tossed the rest of his burger to the dog, locked his car, and set out across the street, up the circular driveway, and into the entrance.

His room reservation was ready, and although the inflated rates at resort casino hotels always irritated him, Andy enjoyed using his new credit card to pay the bill. This was the third time he had used it. The first was for his airline ticket and the second time was for the rental car. He'd never rented a car before. You can't rent a car without a credit card, and this card had been hard for Andy to get. They turned down his application several times, not approving it until after he was in his job for two years. He had smiled at their timing. The credit card arrived in the mail the same day he walked out of Arcade Systems International, leaving the job that he'd needed so much when he got it, that he needed to get the credit card, and which gave birth to the plan and opportunity to its implementation. The credit card would be a big help. He was traveling a lot now. He did not want to carry much cash, and it was convenient to be able to rent a car at last.

The desk clerk spoke acceptable English and was friendly and helpful. He hoped Señor Watson would enjoy his stay. Was this Señor Watson's first visit to Puerto Rico? No? Well perhaps a five-dollar chip on the house would express the management's gratitude that he had chosen the Sands.

Andy had been in Puerto Rico several times in the years that he was self-employed and free-spirited. He'd spent many a long weekend taking in the beach, doing some gambling, roaming around Old San Juan, and buying drinks for the hookers at the Black Angus. If one of them took his fancy, he'd pop for the fifty bucks that bought a half hour in an upstairs room. The AIDS scare had curtailed that last indulgence, and the hard times that came with the decline of his business had stopped the excursions altogether. Now he was back.

The room at the Sands was small but comfortable. He stayed there long enough to shower, shave, and change into a polo shirt and white slacks. He approved of his new image in the mirror. The long hair and beard had given way to a conventional haircut and a small, well-tended mustache. At forty-four and with the new clothes and grooming he looked like a tourist Yuppie from the mainland, just the effect he hoped would make him blend in. Andy did not want to be noticed or remembered. He was about to make his second hit of a gambling casino in as many months.

Years before, Andy had returned home to Shenandoah, Pennsylvania from Vietnam at twenty-two after two years in the brush. He brought with him a taste for alcohol and marijuana and no particular skills except those of a jungle guerrilla fighter. The war had interrupted a boring and undistinguished college career at Penn State, a career he did not feel compelled to resume.

After he returned, he knocked around for two years taking odd jobs bartending, pumping gas, selling one thing and another, and not caring much about the future. If his relaxed attitude about his destiny bothered him at all, he chased the worry away by getting drunk. But the lack of worry was eventually replaced by boredom. Andy got bored with what he was doing both professionally and on his time off. He started looking around for better ways to spend his time.

One day he clipped a coupon in a veteran's magazine. The ad promised free home-assembly kits for a color TV and some electronic test equipment. His veteran's benefits would pay for a correspondence course in electronics, and the course included the kits. He didn't have a TV, and the course looked interesting, so he mailed the coupon.

Two weeks later the first installment arrived, and Andy's life was off in a new direction. Building the test equipment and TV and taking the course was a snap. He was through it in no time at all, discovering aptitude, skills, and interests he didn't know he had.

With the correspondence course done, Andy looked for something else to keep his mind alive. He searched for a way to turn his new interests into a way to make a living, to free him from the daily rut that making a living created. Before long he hit on a plan to turn his new talent into money. He talked some of his veteran friends into signing up for the course. For a small fee, Andy would copy his own test answers onto their lesson tests and build the hardware for them. When he was done, the veteran had a new color TV and a worthless diploma, and Andy had some pocket money. He made a few extra dollars by selling the digital multi-meters, oscilloscopes, and signal and color bar generators that came with the courses. He liked this way of life. To meet more veterans he joined the Amvets, the VFW, and the American Legion and, for a time, business flourished.

One morning he woke up, rushed through a hasty breakfast, eager to get into the makeshift workshop he'd set up in the second bedroom of his apartment. As he plugged in the solder station and turned on the scope and signal generator, he realized that he hadn't smoked a joint or gotten drunk in two weeks. Without intending it, Andy had changed the pattern of his life.

That same day, the mailman brought the first installment of the correspondence course for the latest of Andy's veteran recruits. The package included promotional literature for a new correspondence course on microcomputer maintenance. Students of the new course would get a personal computer kit to build. Andy was running out of friends to build TVs for, and he saw a new opportunity. Finding veterans who wanted home computers was no problem, and before long Andy was building computers.

The little side business had a major impact on Andy's life and direction. From his new-found aptitude and interest, he became a compulsive computer hobbyist, learning how to build and fix the hardware and learning how to design, write, and debug small computer programs. He read everything he could find on the subject and spent all his extra time experimenting with the techniques and methods that he read about in books and magazines.

Andy soon augmented his one-man veteran's benefits program with a small computer repair practice. He helped computer hobbyists get their home-brewed hardware and software working. The little practice grew into a consulting business when local companies began to use small computers. The age of the personal computer had begun and most of the users of the small systems needed help. For a while, Andy did pretty well.

In the eighties, Andy's list of clients dwindled. Businesses began to buy appliance computers from suit-and-tie salesmen in showroom stores. Software came in shrink-wrapped, silk-screened, typeset packages with toll-free 800 numbers for support and money-back guarantees. The torn T-shirt, beard, and blue jeans were no longer welcome in the offices and workplaces of Andy's clients, and Andy found himself going broke. Reluctantly, he decided that he needed a job.

After a long and discouraging search, Andy finally found a job in Texas with Arcade Electronics. Most companies had been unimpressed with his appearance and background, preferring more conventional employees with respectable job histories, degrees, and wardrobes. Andy didn't fit the mold most places. By coincidence, the personnel manager and the director of engineering at Arcade were both Viet Nam veterans. They took a liking to Andy and decided to take a chance on him. The company had a relaxed attitude about dress and appearance, and Andy found himself working again with the technology that he loved. At first he worked on the assembly line building video games and slot machines. Later he moved up to the testing and quality assurance department. Ultimately his new job provided the opportunity that led him to where he was now, riding down the elevator at the Sands, heading for the casino and his next high-tech holdup.

The casino's entrance was just past the lobby. It was a huge room with most of the gaming tables and slots in full view of the lounge and restaurant. Gambling was the main attraction of most of the hotels in San Juan. Without it few tourists would come here.

The hotel management wanted their showcase casino to be conspicuous from all public views on the main floor. A sign at the casino's entrance announced that guests may not bring electronic calculators or computers inside. The sign was to thwart any would-be system players. If they only knew, Andy thought.

He went to the change window and traded a traveler's check for 100 silver dollars. He remembered the first time he'd done this, two months ago, using the last of his savings, still not knowing if the plan would work. The hundred was to make it look like he intended to do some serious gambling at the slots. If everything worked, all he really needed was sixteen dollars.

He walked over to where the gaudy slot machines stood in rows and strolled down a row examining the ones that had TV-like screens. He ignored most of the machines, but stopped at the ones with the large color video screens with multi-color displays that simulated the four wheels of a conventional slot machine. When he found the kind of machine that he was looking for, he sat down and took off his watch, placing it carefully on the ledge alongside the slot machine. With one of these machines, a gambler could bet from one to six silver dollars on a single pull of the arm. If you hit the jackpot, the payoff was $10,000 for a one dollar bet and $60,000 for a six dollar bet.

Andy stuffed five silver dollars in his left hand ready to drop them in the slot one at a time. He watched the sweep-second hand on his watch and dropped a dollar into the slot. When the sweep-second hand pointed at the twelve, he pulled the handle. The simulated wheels spun and then stopped one by one, the computer making simulated clunking sounds as each video wheel bounced to a stop. Andy dropped his second silver dollar into the slot and paid close attention to the watch, ignoring the lemons, oranges, bars, or whatever resulted from his pull. When the sweep second hand on the watch pointed to the two, ten seconds after the first pull, Andy pulled again. The third pull was exactly seven seconds after the second. That one gave him a grape cluster in the left video wheel and paid three silver dollars. They clanked into the chute, but Andy paid no attention to his winnings. The fourth pull was 14 seconds after the third. The fifth one was 12 seconds after that. After he pulled the handle the fifth time, Andy immediately moved his attention from the wristwatch and stared intently at the upper right corner of the screen. When the video wheels stopped spinning, a small rectangular display appeared where Andy was watching. It stayed on the screen for a brief time and then went away. 250 milliseconds exactly, Andy knew, one quarter of a second, gone before you noticed it. The momentary rectangle was what computer programmers call a "window." It was white with a black border and had two words inside the border.

"Hello, Andy."

Hello, yourself, thought Andy. He took a deep breath and sat back on the stool for a moment. 10-7-14-12. He had invested two dollars, counting the three he won, to make sure that the computer inside the slot machine was one of his. He had identified himself to the machine with his code, 10-7-14-12, and the machine recognized him. Hello, Andy. Now he could take his time. This was only the third time Andy had worked this magic, and his heart was pounding. Ready for the kill. Five more silver dollars. In reverse this time, 12-14-7-10. Andy played the sequence. This time the window said:

"Go for it"

Taking a deep breath, Andy dropped six silver dollars into the slot and pulled the handle. Timing didn't matter now. The machine had admitted him through its "back door." This was the payoff pull. The video wheels spun. The first one stopped at the bar, then the second, the third, and then the fourth. Four bars. A jackpot. The machine's siren sounded, and the rotating strobe beacon on the top spun and flashed red. The word JACKPOT blinked on and off at the top of the video screen. The number $60,000 flashed in brilliant white digits.

Heads turned, and a few customers came over to see. Some of them hung around to watch. A few others shook their heads and went back to their own machines, apparently feeling that Andy's jackpot had somehow reduced their own chances. An attendant came over and dispassionately filled out a chit on a pad of blanks. She gave the chit to Andy and waited. He examined it, saw that it was made out for $60,000, and nodded. The attendant pulled a key from a retractable key chain at her waist and inserted it into a slot behind the slot machine. When she turned the key, the siren and strobe light stopped. Andy put a silver dollar into the slot machine and pulled the handle to pull off the winner, a convention among slot players. The machine came up with a grape cluster and paid him three dollars. He grinned sheepishly and tried again, this time pulling a bust. The attendant walked away, and one by one the bystanders drifted back to their own machines.

Chit in hand, Andy returned to the change window.

"Chips or a check?" she asked.

"A check." Andy said. She left and returned a minute later with a check. Andy thanked her, signed a receipt, folded the check, stuffed it in his wallet, and headed for the bar and ordered a martini. He sat at the bar, and sipped his drink. As he drank, he looked over it to the end of the bar and stopped cold. There, sitting on the last stool and grinning at him, sat David Bloomer.

Andy was stunned. Why was Bloomer here?

Andy and David had worked side by side at the test bench at Arcade for about a year. David was there when Andy transferred in. During that year they worked together, took coffee breaks together, and usually had lunch together. Andy didn't know much about David and didn't want to know. Like Andy, David was single and lived alone, but he did not share Andy's passion for the technology. David was about ten years younger and was even more unkempt in his appearance than Andy had been. His beard was shaggy and his clothes were usually rumpled and dirty. Even though Andy had developed most of his plan no farther than ten feet from where David worked, Andy had always believed that David had no idea what was going on.

Still grinning, David slid over onto the stool next to Andy. He cocked his head to one side and looked directly into Andy's eyes. "Tell me how you did it," he said.

"Did what?" Andy said, knowing that the jig was probably up.

"Fixed the slot machines. I saw you win that jackpot. I want to know how you fixed it."

Andy sat quietly for a moment staring at David. He wondered how much David knew and wanted to find out before deciding what more to tell him. "What makes you think I fixed anything?"

"Look, Andy, don't lie to me. What do you think brought me here? Not long after you left, I was running the checkout procedures on a production line. One of the machines blinked at me and said, 'Hello, Andy.' That has to mean something."

That had been Andy's one concern — that by random chance someone would pull the handle in the precise timing sequence of his password pattern and see his 250-millisecond window. He had dismissed the possibility as a long shot. Even if it happened, a gambler wouldn`t realize what it meant. Andy hadn't counted on someone at the plant seeing it. What chance coincidence could have shown it to the very person who might assign the window some significance? What dumb luck.

David went on. "I might have missed it, but I happened to be looking at that part of the screen at just the right time. I was converging the CRT, and pulling the handle to see all the different colors. One area on the screen wasn't coming into focus so I was watching there, and that's how I saw it. I figured you'd done something to the machine to make that window pop up, and I wondered what. I never could make it happen again. How'd you do it? You would've had to change the software. The ROM is kept in a vault and some guy in Japan has the source code."

Andy knew this was going to cost him something. He also knew that David lacked the skill to duplicate what he'd done, so there was little harm in telling him roughly how it worked.

"David, you know the procedures. Where do they keep the master copy of the software ROM chips?"

"In the corporate vault. That's why it would be impossible to..."

Andy interrupted, "I don't mean the master copy. Where do they keep the copy that the production runs are made from?"

"In our department. But, Andy, they replace those copies every time they go to a new revision."

"And how often does that happen?"

David`s voice quickened. "I'll be darned. On the average, once every two years. That model has only been updated once, and that was six months before you left. The next update isn't scheduled yet. They won't be changing it for a while. Your modifications, whatever they are, will be in place until then. Son of a gun. You're going to clean up. But how did you do it?"

"I'll tell you if you'll tell me how you found me here."

"Easy. After I stumbled onto your fix to the machine, I tried to look you up. First I found out that you were still living at the same place. Then the bartender at the Legion told me you said something about coming here in the next couple of days. You were at home the night before last. I called and when you answered, I hung up."

"That was you?"

"Yeah. I wasn't going to say anything until I knew were up to. Figured you'd stonewall me, tell me it was my imagination. So I camped outside your place in my van with enough cokes and sandwiches to last a week. Followed you to the airport and saw what gate you went to. Houston to Miami. It followed that you were coming here or going to one of the other islands that has casinos. Given what that bartender told me, I took a chance it would be here. I bought a ticket on the next flight to San Juan, and here I am."

"How'd you know I'd come to the Sands? There are a dozen casinos in San Juan."

"You forget. I used to handle the maintenance data base at Arcade. The dumb sysop never erased my password. I dialed in and looked it up after that bartender said you might be coming here. Only two casinos in Puerto Rico have the model you fixed, and the other one hasn't installed the new ROM upgrade. You'd have wound up here sooner or later. Turns out it was sooner. It's good I staked out your pad and saw you. I wouldn't have known you without the beard."

Andy didn't want to hear the answer to this next question. "So now what? What do you want?"

"Andy, I want in. I can do you a lot of good. I'll keep my job at Arcade and make sure that whatever you did gets done to all the upgrades. My access to the maintenance data base can keep us current on what casinos to hit." David paused. "And I'll keep my mouth shut. We can score every casino that uses Arcade machines. Now what's wrong with having a partner?"

"I'll tell you what's wrong. I've got this thing pretty well scoped out. As long as I don't draw attention to myself, no problem. I'll hit one machine in one casino town every month. Arcade has machines here, in Vegas, and Atlantic City. That's all I knew about distribution when I left, but it's enough. By holding down the hits, the machines won't seem to be paying off more than normal. This much I do know. These casino guys play hard ball. Tip them off and I'm a goner. That's why I'm holding down the hits. And there's no room for a partner."

"But what happens when Arcade releases new firmware?"

"Then I'm out of business. But with a nice retirement nest egg. I can spend the rest of my life doing whatever I want without needing some boring job at some factory. Now what's it going to take to buy you off?"

"Later. First tell me how you did it."

Andy figured he had nothing to lose by telling David about the plan. David already knew too much, and knowing the rest wouldn't hurt anything. Pulling closer and lowering his voice, Andy explained how he first got the idea when he was working on the assembly line. He realized that he could install a software back door into the new version of the firmware with a bit of effort. But the only way to install and test the back door was to be on the test line. He put in for a transfer and then worked hard to prove himself worthy of the reassignment. The managers already liked his work, so he got the first position that came open. As soon as he was working in the test laboratory, he made a copy of the software read-only-memory chip — the ROM — and took it home. Using his home lab, he worked at night, reverse-engineering the ROM by disassembling it into the microprocessor's assembly language. From there he designed a program patch, which he coded and tested at home. Every time the mechanical interface told the microprocessor that the slot machine's handle was pulled, Andy's patch would step in and start a software timer, a countdown of sorts. On the next pull, the patch checked the elapsed time. When the time between pulls matched a value that Andy had programmed, a new constant value was substituted, and the process started over again. If the sequence was interrupted by a time interval that was not in Andy's password sequence, the whole process reset itself and started over. When the sequence completed with no invalid intervals, the back door patch displayed the Hello,

Andy window for 250 milliseconds. Then the sequence reversed itself. After the reversed sequence completed, the patch displayed the Go For It window.

Andy had found the random number generator for the spinning wheel simulations. He patched into the subroutine to insert the code for a bar display for all four drums after all the pull sequences were done. Four bars are a jackpot, and the original program took over and sent messages to the mechanical interface to display the messages, sound the alarm, and turn on the rotating beacon.

Andy got the back door patch working at home by using a second microprocessor to simulate the Arcade mechanical interface. He took the modified ROM chip to work and installed it into a real slot machine on the test line. Then it was a matter of testing his patch and practicing his timed pulls. When every thing worked to his satisfaction, he copied the ROM and substituted his version for the working copy that the lab maintained. He coordinated the substitution with the quality assurance department's acceptance of the new firmware version. Every slot machine that shipped with the new version went out with Andy's back door installed. And multiple sets of the ROM were sent to all the field maintenance people to upgrade the machines that were already installed in casinos. Andy waited a month for the new version to be in place and waiting for him, and then he quit his job.

David was impressed. "One question. How can you tell whether a machine in a casino has been upgraded? The last upgrade didn't make any changes that you can see. The documentation just said that the biases were adjusted to increase the house's odds and that a few bugs were fixed."

"One of those bugs was on the screen. If you look carefully at the blue background in the upper right corner of the screen on a Rev One machine, you'll see one little pixel dot that flashes on and off intermittently. The Japanese programmer fixed that in Rev Two. I look for a machine that doesn't have the bug."

"What numbers did you use for a password interval sequence?"

Andy had been waiting for that one. David didn't have a good poker face, and his increased excitement showed.

"Sorry, David, I think for now I'll keep that information to myself. Now cut to the chase. What do you want?"

"Like I said, I want in. If you won't give me the key to the back door, then cut me in on your take. Fifty-fifty."

"No deal. As I told you before, there isn't enough room in the budget for a full partner."

"That's only because of your conservative approach. Double your hits, and there'd be plenty for both of us."

"I explained that to you. I don't want to draw attention to myself or to the machines. If the casinos figure that those particular slots are paying off too much, they'll start watching them. I'll be seen, and my picture will be all over every casino in every town. They'll send the slots back and somebody will find the back door patch. It all falls down around my shoulders. Even if the company doesn't send me to jail, the casino goons will break my arms and legs. No, I won't increase the hits. And there's no reason to give you half either. I did all the work, and I'm taking all the risks. Why should I give you half?" Andy paused to let his words sink in. Then, "Here's what I will do. Every time I make a hit, starting today, I'll pay you five grand to keep quiet. If that won't do it and you blow the whistle, I'll stop making hits and drop out of sight. They'll think you're nuts."

"How about ten grand."

"Don't get greedy. You can walk out of here with a check for five grand right now, or you can go home broke. One offer is all you get."

"How do I know when you've made a hit?"

"It will average one a month unless I get spooked, in which case I might lay low for a month. It will last as long as I can find my machines out there. I'll send you a check every time I score. In exchange you can root around in that database and make a list of the casinos that have my machine. That'll earn your keep for the five grand and save me some time. That's my offer. Take it or leave it."

"I guess I'll take it." A pause. "Is there any way you could get me some cash today? Since I'm here, I'd like to have some fun."

"Yeah, I`ve got a charge card that will get me a one-grand advance. I'll give you that much in cash and the rest in a check. But keep one thing in mind. This is as far as it goes. Try to squeeze for more, and I'll shut down the enterprise."

Andy wrote the check and used his charge card in one of the teller machines in the casino. It cost one hundred dollars to get a one thousand dollar advance, but he figured it was worth it to get David out of his hair. They parted company in the bar, and Andy went to his room. He put in a wake-up call so he could catch the morning flight back to Houston. Then he went to bed.

Several days later a manilla envelope arrived in Andy's mail in Houston. It contained a computer printout of the casinos in Las Vegas, San Juan, and Atlantic City where Arcade had installed Andy's slot machines with the upgraded ROM. A note from David said that he'd learned from a guy in marketing that they were trying to sell a package into a chain of casinos in Germany. The note ended with, "Want company, pardner?" Andy scowled at David's obvious attempt to get familiar. But then he shrugged it off, and figured it was a small-enough price to pay.

The following month he went to Las Vegas, visiting a different casino than the one he hit his first time out. As before, the back door worked perfectly, and he begrudgingly mailed David a check. A month after that Andy was in Atlantic City. This time, however, there was a difference, one that Andy did not notice. David Bloomer, now minus his beard and in brand new tourist clothes, sat at a table in the lounge and watched Andy make his score, watched him through a pair of field glasses while operating a stopwatch with his other hand.

Another month passed. It was February, and Andy had looked forward to this trip back to San Juan. Houston streets were covered with a thin sheet of ice and the balmy Caribbean weather was a pleasant change. He had made five scores so far totalling $300,000. His travel expenses had been small, and he'd paid $15,000 to David. Even after living expenses he still had well over $250,000. Andy decided to quit the game after he had a million dollars. That would be enough to last the rest of his life no matter where he wanted to live. It would take about another year. He'd stop paying David when he got near his goal. By then he'd have figured out where he wanted to go.

The hits had become routine. His heart no longer pounded when he sat down to score. He could look a cashier or floor attendant squarely in the eye when he collected his winnings. He wouldn't return to San Juan for a while. With only two casinos to hit, someone might remember him.

He ran the silver-dollar sequence up to the Hello, Andy window. As he reached to drop the first silver dollar of the reverse sequence, he felt a firm hand on his shoulder. He looked around to see a tall, well-built, young Puerto Rican man in a black suit, white shirt, and black bow tie standing behind him gripping his shoulder tightly.

"Buenos noches, Señor Watson. Might we have a word with you in the manager's office?" The question's tone implied that it was not intended to be answered, and the invitation was not meant to be refused. The big hand slipped under his arm and lifted him off the stool to his feet. Another man — smaller, older, balding, and wearing the same kind of black suit — rushed up and inserted a key into the back of the machine. When he turned the key, the machine's power shut down and its screen went dark. The smaller man hung an "Out of Order" sign on the machine and hurried off. The first man moved Andy in the direction taken by the older man.

Andy sat on a leather couch facing the manager's ornate walnut desk. The tall young man was standing between him and the closed door with his arms crossed. The older man, apparently the manager, was sitting behind the desk. He was the first to speak.

"We have been waiting for you, Señor Watson. Now we must discuss what it is that we are to do about you."

Andy had no idea how much they knew or what they intended to do to him, but he was sure that David Bloomer figured in somewhere. He tried bluffing it out.

"What do you mean draggin' me in here? You can't treat me like this. I'm an American citizen."

"So are we, Señor Watson. Puerto Rico is a protectorate of the United States and we are all citizens here. We brought you here because you were about to steal $60,000 from us."

"Steal? What are you talking about?"

"You are acquainted with Señor David Bloomer?"

"Yeah. So what?" Andy's heart sank.

"Señor Bloomer was detained by the security forces of a casino in Las Vegas last month. He had just won the fourth jackpot in a row from their slot machines. All four were the same kind of slot machine, and he won those jackpots all in the same night."

"Stupid jerk," Andy muttered.

"Yes, I agree. It seems that every time he won, he'd take his winnings in chips and proceed to lose it all at the crap table. Whenever he would run out of money he'd go and collect another jackpot. Naturally they got suspicious. Señor Bloomer was not entirely sober when he did all this. I suspect that he sobered up rather quickly when they picked him up."

"What did he tell them?"

"He did not implicate you, Señor Watson. He described the little modifications that you made to our equipment, but he took the credit for himself. I heard that after that, he attempted to sell them his services as an expert consultant in the field of electronic security. Unsuccessfully, I might add."

"They let him go?"

"They talked to his employer, who notified us and the other casinos. Everyone agreed to avoid the negative publicity that this incident would generate. Arcade does not want potential new customers to know that such a penetration was made or could be made by one of its employees, and the management of the casinos do not want the public to believe that their gaming facilities can be fixed in any way."

"So where is David now?"

"Probably out looking for a job somewhere. Your former employer did not believe that Señor Bloomer possesses the skills required to implement such a scheme. A 'back door,' I believe they called it. Curious phrase. However, they did identify the only other person in their organization who could have made such a thing happen. That would be you, of course. They sent us the picture from your personnel records. Allow me to say that you look better without the beard and long hair. Apparently, just before he resigned, Señor Bloomer prepared a database list of casinos where the offending slot machines are installed. They tell me that his unauthorized use of their database left an audit trail which they discovered. The casinos on that list have been watching the slot machines that you modified. Until now, that is. We've already faxed the others that we have you here. We waste little time."

"So what happens to me."

"You are completely and forevermore out of business, Mr Watson. You will find another way to make your living. We do not know how much money you made from this enterprise or from which casinos you made it, so there will be no retributions, but we very definitely do not care to see you again in our establishments. In a few minutes Eddie here will take you to have a picture made of you and your new look. You should cooperate. It's us or the police. I can assure you that from this day forward, your patronage will be most unwelcome in any of the casinos in the Western world."

"No broken limbs? No concrete overshoes? I thought you guys played rougher than that."

"You have been seeing too many movies, Señor Watson. But please do not tempt us. Now that we have located and properly identified you, Arcade will be replacing the parts you modified with copies made from their master program. You may go on your way. The hotel management knows nothing of this matter, so stay as long as you wish. I am sure you can afford it. Only do not return to this or any other casino, please."

The manager gestured to the young man named Eddie who then escorted Andy out of the office and to the entrance of the casino.

Seven months passed while Andy laid low. He heard nothing from or about David, and no one from Arcade made any effort to contact him or do anything about his escapades with their equipment. After a time he relaxed and thought about getting on with life. He considered getting another job, but anything that was suited to his abilities seemed tame after his somewhat reckless entrepreneurial activities. Then something in the paper caught his attention. He fabricated a resume and wrote a letter. A week later he had an invitation to come to Florida for interviews.

Now Andy nervously rolled and unrolled the employment application in his hands as he fidgeted on the uncomfortable steel and vinyl waiting room couch. He didn't really need this job, but the idea of working here had intrigued him ever since he saw the help-wanted ad in the Houston newspaper. They were looking for systems programmers to work in Tallahassee, Florida. He'd been expecting the details of his past to surface during their background check, but apparently Arcade kept their word and omitted any reference to Andy's failed plan.

The new suit was uncomfortable, and he couldn't wait to take the tie off. One more interview to go. He was sure he'd get this job. He unrolled the application form and read again the heading at the top of the first page:

Application for Employment
State of Florida
Department of Revenue
State Lottery Commission

The Store

The computer's video screen glowed with little letters and numbers, forming orderly rows and columns that described and enumerated the financial condition of Miller's Music Store. Without interpretation, the spreadsheet meant nothing, just numbers. But to the eye of a person schooled in business administration they spelled one thing: impending failure. Rich Miller did not have the education, but he knew what the numbers meant. He'd been seeing this crash coming for months. He was, in fact, its architect. A one-time jazz trumpet player and now the sole proprietor of this small music store in a small Virginia town, Rich Miller knew enough about business—his business—to see the inevitable. Damn computer. It had no soul and it didn't care. My ax never talked to me like this, he thought.

Rich was in his late forties, tall, balding, slightly over-weight, a neat mustache. Among friends he talked in the hip jargon that hinted at his past. With customers he dropped the slang and assumed a business-like manner intended to impress them and make a sale. Rich had played and taught music most of his life. In the early days in New York he had been well-received as an up-and-coming jazz personality. With a few recordings to his credit in the company of some well-known jazz artists, he had spent several summers in Europe, booking himself into the small clubs in France, Germany, and Switzerland, where his reception as a died-in-the-wool American jazz musician had given him some of the happiest times of his life. He enjoyed this small success for a while, but the pressures of travel and the night life were too much for him. Alcohol and drugs were too close, too good, and too threatening, and he dropped out while he was still able, in the nick of time, he thought. He came out with some money, reasonably straight, not addicted to anything, and able to manage his own life. He moved to a small southern town and opened a music store.

Most jazz musicians dream of someday owning a bar or a music store. The ones who perform for a living usually want a bar. Those who teach or sell instruments in a daytime job—a day gig—tend to want a store. In either case they see themselves running a business the right way, doing things the way they always knew things should be done. Some of them realize those dreams and open that store or bar, and almost always it changes them. They become the kind of owner that they despised, although most of them do not see it happening. Rich refused to let that happen to him. He opted for the store rather than the bar for the same reasons he had given up a full-time playing career. He didn't want to be that close to the lower elements and influences of his former profession. And so Rich did not become the kind of store owner that he had always criticized. He ran his store the way he wanted to run it, the way he knew it should be run. He was fair with his employees and his customers. For several years, it had worked well.

Now there was a recession. People stopped buying pianos and organs. He sold an occasional guitar, and the annual tour of high schools to sell band instruments would keep things going for a while, but that was several months away. Rich had a cash problem. What was worse, he had an inventory problem, and it was about to catch up with him.

When he started out, Rich had bought and sold used instruments. He gave some lessons, kept a modest rack of sheet music, and maintained a small inventory of incidentals—reeds, mouthpieces, valve oil, staff paper, all the stuff that musicians use. He saw his store as a hangout for professional musicians. Although he was happy to cater to the casual amateur, Rich preferred providing for his peers, the professionals. There were not so many of them in this small Virginia town, and although the jazz players from Washington, D.C., the only nearby city, knew and respected him, they rarely made the forty mile drive south to his place any more. But his business grew slowly, and gradually he changed its emphasis, finding a certain satisfaction in buying and selling used pianos, guitars, and band instruments.

One day Rich was visited by the Kawai representative. Kawai made pianos, and they had no dealers in Rich's area except for a music store at the mall. They wanted a presence in the quaint, downtown area as well.

Rich told them that he couldn't afford to stock his store with enough new pianos to offer the kind of image that Kawai wanted. Not to worry, said the rep, we'll give you a floor plan. What's a floor plan? Simple, replied the rep. Kawai loans you the pianos. You pay prime rate on the wholesale value of the inventory. When you sell a piano, you pay it off, and we replace it. You, of course, keep the markup, which, if you do a proper job of selling and turn inventory over at a good rate, more than covers the interest you'll be paying and makes you a profit. As your business grows, you increase the size of your floor plan. Most businesses with an inventory line do it—car dealers, furniture stores, computer stores, virtually every chain music store. Nothing to it.

Nothing to it? Sure, when folks are buying pianos, which they did for a while. Most people wanted to finance their purchase, and Rich found another opportunity in this side of the business. The banks gave cash incentives to merchants who wrote commercial loans so customers could finance their purchases. Rich soon had a working relationship with several banks in the county. He would prepare and submit a loan application, and when the bank approved the loan, Rich collected the money from the bank and delivered the piano to the customer. He could make it very easy for a customer to buy with nothing down. He'd write the loan application for the discounted sale price of the piano and write the sales contract as if the customer had paid the difference between the sale and list prices as a down payment. The bank didn't care. In fact, it was a banker who suggested it to him in the first place. The buyer gets the loan approved, and the bank has the title to the piano for collateral. Nobody ever defaults on a piano. The banks never even bothered to verify that the piano was delivered. As long as the buyer made the payments, the system worked. Everything went well for a while. Then the recession came.

In a recession people stop buying things they don't need. Rich didn't understand what starts a recession but he could see it feed on itself. The slowdown in purchases caused reductions in production, transportation, and distribution, all of which cost jobs, which further reduced spending. People who are worried about losing their jobs don't buy what they can do without. Everyone can do without a piano. Sales fell off dramatically. The recession got worse.

It cost Rich $3500 every month to keep the store open. That included his rent, the utilities, and the interest on the floor plan. He had let go his two salesmen and the bookkeeper months before. He was doing everything himself, even sweeping the floor. If he sold a piano, he had to pay a tuner and a mover, and Kawai got the wholesale cost of the piano out of the proceeds. He needed to sell ten pianos a month to stay ahead. But he wasn't selling anywhere near that. Three or four a month was about average.

Something had to give. About the same time he cut his staff, he stopped paying Kawai when he sold a piano. He kept up the interest payments because they'd come get the rest of the pianos if he didn't. But since they never visited his store, he didn't bother telling them when he sold a piano. He figured that if he sold one for $4000, that money kept him in business for another month and left him $500 to live on. The recession couldn't last forever. He'd catch up when business picked up. Gradually, though, his inventory dwindled and he just barely kept going. His store lost credibility. Customers saw that he didn't have a selection any more. That further contributed to the sales decline. The chains could throw cash at the problem and wait it out. Rich couldn't. Just like the recession, Rich's business slump was feeding on itself.

Now, Rich sat in the small office he kept at the back of the store and stared at the computer spreadsheet screen that described his circumstance. There was no getting around it. Short of a miracle, he'd have to close his doors at the end of this month. There was every chance that Kawai could bring criminal charges of fraud against him. Certainly they'd get whatever else he still owned, which wasn't very much. He couldn't even afford a lawyer to tell him what was going to happen to him. No question about it, Rich needed a miracle. If Kawai walked in today and audited his books, they'd find out that after they took his remaining inventory, he would still owe them roughly $80,000. They'd also find out that he was broke.

The entrance bell rang to announce that a customer was coming in. Rich turned off the computer with its indifferent bad news, and went out into the showroom. A small, elderly, well-dressed man stood in the middle of the room looking around at the few pianos that were left. Rich turned on his broad, winning smile, the one he reserved for potential customers, and greeted the newcomer.

"Good morning, sir. And how may we help you today?"

"Yes, I am interested in purchasing a grand piano." The little man spoke with a hesitance, as if he expected to be contradicted and wanted to have a tone of apology in place, in advance.

"Well sir, this is the right place. We have a really nice five-foot walnut Kawai over here."

"No, I'm looking for something quite different."

The five-foot was the last grand in Rich's inventory. This guy wants a different one. No one buys a piano sight unseen, and Rich didn't want to call Kawai's attention to his situation by ordering something they thought he still had. Got to point this customer in another direction.

"Perhaps you are looking for something smaller. Or a used piano. I have several used grands that I've taken in trade. They're all in the shop being reconditioned just now, but I could arrange to show you one later." A lie. Rich didn't have any used grands. But, given a buyer, he'd rustle one up in a hurry, even if he had to get it out of the classified ads.

The old man was looking at a scrap of note paper that he had taken from his pocket. "No, I want a new piano. I know exactly what I want, and I'm looking for someone locally who carries it. Do you handle Bosendorfer pianos?"

Rich's heart skipped a beat. He swallowed and concentrated on what his expression must be revealing, consciously working to correct the image he projected. Bosendorfer is the Rolls Royce of pianos. Very expensive, very exclusive. Few American dealers handle the line because you don't sell many of them and the floor plan cost is high. You have a Bosendorfer on the floor only for the image, and not many piano dealers can afford image these days. This guy wants a Bosendorfer? You bet I carry Bosendorfer. Another lie coming.

"Why, yes I do. I just sold my last model a few days ago, and the next shipment is due soon. We had a clearance sale. That's why there isn't much stock just now."

Rich thought fast. How long will it take me to get a Bosendorfer? What is the longest delay I can sell this guy without him walking out.

He remembered a book about selling. The book said to imagine a bag of groceries where the customer's head is. Concentrate on that bag of groceries. To eat tonight, you have to make that sale. "Are you in a rush to get the piano?" he asked the bag of groceries.

"No, the piano is for my daughter. She is quite an accomplished pianist, and she'll be going away to school next month. She's taking her Steinway with her, and we want her to have a good instrument here at home for when she has time off. She says Bosendorfer is the best, so that's what I want." He looked at the paper. "The nine-foot model. Ebony. How soon can you have one?"

"I'll have to check the delivery schedule. Of course, you'll need to try it out before you decide? Your daughter will want to play it?"

"No, if you have one, I'll buy it. It's a surprise. What do I know about pianos? I want what it says here on the paper. A nine-foot ebony Bosendorfer."

Nine-foot. Big bucks. There's caviar in that bag of groceries. Rich talked fast. "Can you give me some time to get in touch with the distributor and see when they can have one here? A couple of hours. Then I can tell you the price, too. The prices change practically every day. Something about fluctuations in the exchange rate. I don't really understand how all that works, but it does."

"Well, I'll pay whatever it costs. You're a local business, established, well recommended by a banker I know. He says I can trust you. You won't try to bamboozle me. You'll make me a good price."

"Well. Thank you very much. Who is your banker if I might ask? We like to know who says good things about us."

"Dan Burley at the First. He's not my banker, but we are acquainted. He suggested I come here."

"Yes, I know him. Fine fellow. We play golf. Now, what about financing? The Bosendorfer is an expensive piano. If you'd care to take a loan application with you, I can process it through several banks until I find one that will accept the application. That would save you the trouble."

"That would be convenient," said the man. "How much money are we talking about? More than twenty thousand?"

"Definitely more than that. Quite a bit more. I'll have an exact figure for you later."

Rich went into his office and brought several loan application blank forms out to the customer. The man gave him a card, thanked him, and left. Rich watched through the glass of the the front door as the little man crossed the street and got into a Mercedes. Rich read the card. Buford Prentice. The name meant nothing. Rich went back into his office and flipped his Rolodex to the First Federal Savings and Loan, dialed the number, and asked for Dan Burley, the president.

"Dan, who is Buford Prentice? He says you recommended me."

"Yeah, I did. Nice guy. He's a manager for the fuel oil distributorship. Handles several counties."

"Can he afford a really expensive piano?"

"I would think so. His business is fairly sound. The recession doesn't cut into fuel oil. People still get cold, and Prentice runs a tight operation, I'm told, and gets pretty good bonuses in addition to salary. He travels in different circles than you do. You really ought to join the Chamber, Rich. You'd meet some of these guys."

"He'd have no sweat getting a loan, then? For the piano, I mean. It's a lot of scratch."

"A loan? No problem. His credit should be good anywhere. I'd think he'd pay cash, though. He doesn't bank here, so I don't know his financial picture."

"This particular piano is going to be in the neighborhood of fifty, sixty grand, Dan. Mr. Prentice took a loan application with him, so I assume he doesn't have that kind of dust laying around." Rich probed a little. "I thought I'd check with you since you banker guys get tense about commercial loans that big."

"That's for sure. Prentice should be OK, though. Everyone I know respects him. Be sure to send us the application. I'd like to get some of his business."

"I will. We haven't gotten that far yet. I just wanted to make sure he could afford the box before I go out on a limb and get one in here. Thanks for the heads up. I'll call you later."

After several phone calls, Rich located the east coast Bosendorfer representative. He expected to run into problems ordering a piano with no relationship with the company and not being a well-known chain. At best, they'd want cash on delivery; at worst, they'd demand cash with order before they'd ship. That would mean getting a short-term loan based on the order, and he didn't think he could get one given the current state of his finances. But Rich's fears were unfounded. Bosendorfer had been wanting dealer representation in the area for a long time. The little town was a minor cultural center with its own community symphony and a prestigous young woman's finishing school, just the place to have their company's line of fine pianos in evidence. Bosendorfer had tried to penetrate most of the chain music stores in the nearby malls and had struck out. All the dealers were playing it close to the vest until things picked up. Besides, most of them had exclusive agreements with other manufacturers that prevented them from carrying competing lines.

Rich's timing was good. Better than good, it was perfect. He had a sure sale of a high-ticket item that no other dealer in the area would carry. Buford Prentice wouldn't find a Bosendorfer anywhere else. Those mall organ store managers wouldn't have the balls to bluff it out and get one the way he was doing. Before he got around to telling the Bosendorfer rep about the sale to Buford, the rep was offering to put the piano of Rich's choice on his floor plan at two points under prime with the first three months interest-free, and they'd pay for the shipment. All Rich needed was a local business reference. Rich gave the guy Dan Burley's name and number and told him to get a nine-foot ebony grand ready to ship.

He hung up the phone and turned the computer back on. Using the pricing information that the Bosendorfer guy gave him, he added the potential sale to his spreadsheet. It was going to work. He stood to make a $38,000 profit if he sold the piano at the $70,000 list price. He could coast on that amount for ten months, longer if sales picked up, plenty of time for the economy to turn around. He could gamble on a shorter time for the economic recovery and pay off some of the Kawais to get replacements in the showroom. Rich Miller had needed a miracle, and someone or something had sent him good ol' Buford Prentice.

The next morning, Buford Prentice returned. He had the loan application filled out, and Rich told him that the piano would be delivered within the week. Rich made up a sales contract at the $70,000 list price. Prentice asked for a discount, and they agreed on $65,000 with a $5,000 down payment. Prentice wrote a check for $500 for a deposit, and filled in a loan amount of $60,000 on the application. After Prentice left, Rich looked at the loan application. The guy's financial situation was impressive, for sure. He had plenty of savings, some real estate, and a six-figure income. Rich knew from years of handling these applications that Prentice could afford the payments as far as the banks were concerned. There would be no problem getting approval for this one. He had made five copies of the application to take to the five banks he usually did business with. He figured he'd give Dan Burley's bank first crack at it, but it wouldn't hurt to submit the application to more than one bank. He closed the store at lunch time and delivered the application to the officers of all five banks in person. Most of them raised their eyebrows at the size of the loan, but they all promised they'd run it through their loan approval committees. Dan Burley as much as told Rich the loan was approved in advance. Things were on the mend for Miller's Music Store.

The Bosendorfer arrived three days later. It was magnificent. Rich was no pianist, but he knew a few chords, and when he gently pressed the keys, the store filled with glorious sound. He made two calls. The first was to Roger, the only tuner that Rich respected within three states. Roger would be over in two hours to fine-tune the Bosendorfer, supervise its move, and tune it again after it was delivered. The second call was to Prentice to arrange delivery. Rich had approvals from four of the five banks for the loan. Prentice said he could accept delivery any evening that week. And one thing more. He wouldn't need the loan. He'd be paying the $64,500 balance by check upon delivery.

While Roger was inspecting and admiring the finest piano he had ever seen, Rich sat at his computer playing what-if games with the spreadsheet. He tried all the options. He could pay Bosendorfer for the piano and use his profit to operate for a while. He could use part of the profit to pay off some of the long-gone Kawais and replenish his stock. Once, for grins, he ran a scenario where he said to hell with them all, closed the doors, and took the $65,000 with him into the sunset. He wasn't serious about it, though. Keeping the store open and beating these hard times meant a lot more to him than the prospect of living it up for a while as the fugitive from a white-color crime.

That was when the call came in. It hit him like a brick. The Kawai representative would be visiting the store the day after tomorrow. Their analysis of his sales did not fit the profile that their computer model predicted for his territory even in light of the current economic picture. Mr. Kurihara would like to audit the books, take an inventory, and discuss the withdrawal of the Kawai franchise from Miller's Music Store. The bomb had just dropped.

There was no way around it. Rich was in deep trouble. He hung up the phone and looked again at the whimsical game he had been playing with the computer. It didn't look so whimsical now. He turned it off and went out to the floor to see how things were coming with the Bosendorfer. They were ready to go. The big ebony beast was on its side with its legs removed and its pedals tucked into its belly. It was wrapped with mover's pads and strapped to a skid board ready for the trip into the van and out to the Prentice residence. Roger was helping the movers lift it and slide the dolly under the skid board. Rich grabbed the sales contract and followed them through the storage room in back to the loading dock. He watched them load the piano and then went to his car to lead the way to Prentice's house.

The next day Rich went to the bank and deposited the check. His own bank was the one that he hadn't heard from about Prentice's loan application. While he was there, the loan officer who had taken the application came out and handed him their approval. Not necessary, Rich told him, and left the bank to return to the store. Now he had to deal with the matter of the Kawai representative. There seemed to be no way out. His spreadsheets offered no solution. Every now and then he returned to the one that he had filled out on a lark. Then he looked down at his desk where the four approved loan applications for $65,000 lay waiting to be discarded. He turned back to the spreadsheet on the screen, typed a few strokes, and called up his bank balance. He had deposited Prentice's $500 deposit and the $64,500 payoff that he collected when he delivered the piano. A check to Roger for $200 had settled the account for tuning and moving. With the small balance he had before and a few paltry receipts in the past few days, his balance was now $64,947.22.

Rich fixed his stare onto the screen. He could see his reflection dimly behind the rows and columns of dots that formed the numbers and letters of the spreadsheet. He wasn't sure he knew the face of desperation that stared back at him from behind the source of its plight. Shaking the doubt from his head and focusing back on the surface of the screen, he changed the computer to run the program that printed the installment sales contracts. He prepared four of them, each one showing a different bank as the mortgagor. After practicing the forgery on some scratch paper, he signed Prentice's name to each of the contracts. Then he prepared the four documents that represented the title to the piano. He had been making these on his laser printer for years. The banks wanted them for their records. They meant nothing, but they looked official. He picked up the four loan applications, clipped each to its corresponding loan approval along with one of the titles, and went out again. He drove to each of the four banks and exchanged the loan packages for certified checks made out to Miller's Music Store for $60,000 each. His last stop was at his bank where he deposited the four checks. Back at the store, he added the new deposits to his bank account spreadsheet and read the new balance: $304,947.22. He dialed the number of the travel agent next door. Then he made an overseas call to the bank in Switzerland where his agent of several years ago had done business.

The next morning Rich went to the store to pick up a few personal belongings: his trumpet; his passport; a few letters from fans and club owners in Europe; his address book from back then. He looked around at the few pianos that were left, the sheet music rack, the display case with the reeds and valve oil laid out neatly in rows. He hung out the Closed sign, turned off the lights, locked the doors, and left.

The account manager at his bank believed his story about selling the business, which would account for the large deposit yesterday. The fool didn't wonder why a business that had an average balance of less than two hundred dollars for several months was now worth $240,000, and he didn't notice that the deposit was from checks drawn on four different local banks. The transfer of funds from his account to the bank in Switzerland took about an hour. Four hours later he intentionally parked his rattletrap in a parking space reserved for members of Congress at Washington National Airport and said goodbye to the car, to his country, and to its recession.

The Cat, the Computer and the Cuckoo

Little Bill Palmer jiggled the joystick control on his wheelchair to pull away from the dinner table. The electric motor made a whirring noise as it moved the chair backward and rotated Bill toward the door that led from the dining room into the hallway. Little Bill's mother quietly watched her son as she had done every day for the past twenty-three years. His mobility was vastly enhanced by the devices that helped him now, but he was still as personally limited as he had always been.

Susie, Little Bill's small Siamese cat, jumped into his lap as soon as he was clear of the table. She was his perpetual companion, always with him except when he ate dinner. His mother loved the little cat but did not want it at the dinner table, so although Susie spent most of the day in Little Bill's lap or running around the wheels of his chair, and although she slept with him every night, she knew that when Little Bill went to dinner, she could not go with him. She had learned to jump down when the chair approached the table and knew that her own dish would be ready in the kitchen while he ate. After her evening meal she would curl up in a corner of the kitchen and wait. As soon as she heard the whir of the wheelchair motor, she was back in the dining room in a flash, ready to jump into his lap when the wheelchair was clear of the table.

His father had nicknamed him Little Bill when he was small. True to the name, he had never gotten very big. Cerebral palsy had inhibited his growth as it does most of its victims because it inhibits the body movements that promote growth. Little Bill could move his head and his right arm and hand. Everything else was paralyzed. It was difficult for him to hold his head upright, and it tended to fall off to one side or another, so he had learned to let it fall and then view everything from a slanted perspective. His intellect and sense of humor were, however, in place and operating, unaffected by his disability. Little Bill's I.Q. had been measured well above the genius level. His speech was labored and slurred, but his thoughts were clear and organized. He read—or his mother read to him—every book that came into the house. She started reading to him long before anyone knew that he understood. She had fought to find a place for him in the state educational system when they insisted that he should go to a school for the mentally retarded. Winning that battle, she had seen to it that his life and education were as normal as possible, and she had remained his staunchest advocate all his life. Now an adult, Little Bill was mostly confined to his home with his mother as his best friend and caretaker and Susie as his constant companion. His father had died a few years before but not before planning for and securing their futures with an adequate insurance program. Little Bill had a trust fund that would take care of him the rest of his life, and because of it his mother did not need to work. By choice, she devoted her life to him.

A year before, Little Bill's mother had bought him a personal computer after he read about them and expressed his interest. He picked out what he wanted from the magazines he read, and his mother bought it and had the local computer store people deliver and install it. She had them arrange it on his reading desk at just the correct angle so that he could reach the keyboard with his right hand as he viewed the screen. She hoped the computer would broaden his exposure to things that he could read and learn.

Little Bill's first computer opened a world to him that he otherwise could never have known. By using his modem, he began to communicate with other computer users in the on-line community—people who signed onto electronic bulletin boards and on-line services every day throughout the country. To this new circle of friends, Little Bill became simply Bill, and to them he was normal. There was no reason for any of his electronic correspondents to know about his handicap. They could not see his chair, observe his paralysis, or hear his labored speech. None of them could tell that it took him a long time to type with his one good hand the short messages he sent to them. For the first time in his life he was able to communicate with people without being afforded special consideration. For the first time, no one gave him extra measure or made extra effort to be agreeable. No one went out of their way to be nice to him just because he was handicapped. And, for the first time, no one automatically assumed that his opinions and abilities were somehow bounded because of the limited view of the world that they thought his disability afforded.

When he realized the potential of this new form of communication, Little Bill was hooked. He spent all his spare time exchanging messages with his on-line friends. After a time, he decided to expand this new circle of friends by installing and operating his own electronic bulletin board. To that end, his mother bought him a second computer, had it installed, and arranged for the additional phone lines he needed. He got enough public-domain software to set himself up as a "sysop," the system operator of a BBS—bulletin board service—and his new computer went on line as the BBBB service, or Big Bill's Bulletin Board. With BBBB in operation, many other computer users would now call his service. The board had been installed and operating for one week, and Little Bill was pleased with the response from the on-line community. There was one problem, though. The new computer and Little Bill's cuckoo clock were not getting along.

Susie curled up on Little Bill's lap as he motored down the hall and into the small room that was his private study. All his treasured possessions were in this room, and, except for at dinner time and when he was sleeping, Little Bill spent most of his hours here. His mother served his breakfast and lunch to him at one of his computers, but she insisted that he take dinner at the dining room table. One wall of his study was lined with book cases. Little Bill could reach only two of the shelves, but his mother was on constant call to come and retrieve anything that he might want from one of the higher or lower shelves.

Bill's clock collection decorated the other walls. He was proud of the collection of regulator and chime wall clocks that his father had left him. His pride and joy was a Black Forest cuckoo clock that occupied a place of honor on the wall above his BBS computer. Every eight days, his mother dutifully wound all the clocks. She would have to pull the weights on the cuckoo clock more often now because they no longer reached the floor—the new computer was in the way.

As he maneuvered the chair into the study, Little Bill saw what he expected he'd see, what he'd seen every evening since he had installed the new computer. The cuckoo clock was stopped at six o'clock and so was the computer. Since he'd installed the BBS, his two favorite possessions had shut down at exactly the same time every evening. He wheeled over to the BBS computer and pressed the Enter key. The BBS started running again. Any callers who had been on-line at six o'clock had hung up, and the computer, being stopped, had refused to answer any more calls since then. Now, with one press of the key, the BBS was running perfectly again. This was, indeed, very mysterious. He pressed the intercom button on his wheelchair and called his mother. In a few seconds she was at the door.

"What is it, Bill?"

"The clock and the computer stopped again."

Little Bill's mother did not understand computers and assumed that they could stop whenever they pleased for any reason at all, so that was no mystery to her. But the business about the clock was a puzzle. Why did it stop every day at six o'clock, and why only since the new computer came into the house? Little Bill had explained to her that no one calling his computer could tell it to shut down, and they certainly could not tell the clock to stop, so she was unable to explain to her own satisfaction what was happening. Her first suggestion was to send the clock to the clock shop and the computer to the computer shop, but Little Bill figured both repairmen would only laugh. No, this was a mystery that he had to solve himself. His mother touched the cuckoo clock's pendulum to start it swinging again, reset the hands to the correct time, and walked out shaking her head. This mystery was making her son unhappy, and an adult lifetime of looking after his needs conditioned her to want very much to do something about it. But she did not know what to do.

The following evening, Little Bill asked if he could eat dinner an hour later than usual. He stationed himself at the door of his study and watched the computer and the cuckoo clock from 5:45 until 6:15. Susie shared his vigil from his lap offering an occasional meow and a constant purr for company. Nothing unusual happened, and both devices continued to work normally. He had his dinner and returned to find that the clock and the computer had delayed their mutual shutdown just as he had delayed his dinner. Both devices stopped at seven instead of at six. The mystery was now more of a puzzle. It was as if the clock and the computer knew when he was watching.

For several days he changed his dinner time every evening. His mother patiently agreed to support this erratic pattern if he promised it would be short-lived. She did not want her son's frail health threatened by drastic changes in his nutritional schedule. But the unpredictable dinner hour did not fool whatever unknown force was invading Little Bill's study. No matter what time he ate, the cuckoo clock and computer shut down on the hour during his meal.

As an experiment, Little Bill stopped the computer himself just before dinner one evening. On schedule, the clock stopped at six. The next evening he left the computer running and had his mother stop the clock. When he looked in after dinner, the computer was still running. This was strange, indeed. It seemed that the cuckoo clock was stopping the computer but only when the clock itself was running.

The next morning Little Bill made an announcement. "Mother, it's time for some electronic surveillance. We must buy a video camcorder."

Never denying her son any reasonable request, his mother finished her morning chores, wheeled him outside to the modified minivan with the wheelchair lift, and drove him to the mall. As usual, Bill would not allow her to park in a handicapped space even though the van's license plate displayed the required sticker. According to Bill, someone who really needed the space might come along. He'd rather park farther away and motor his wheelchair from the parking lot to the mall entrance. After searching all the stores that carried camcorders, Little Bill selected one, and his mother bought it. They took it home and she removed it from its package and set it up in his study while Susie watched and he read aloud the instructions about its installation and placement. When she was done, the camcorder was in a position to observe the activities of the study with the computer and cuckoo clock in full view of the camcorder's lens.

Little Bill could hardly wait for dinner time. When at last his mother called him, he rolled over to where the camcorder waited and pressed the record button. Then he went to dinner as usual. As usual, Susie scampered out of his lap and off to the kitchen for her meal. When dinner was over, Little Bill eagerly wheeled into the study. Sure enough the computer and the cuckoo clock were stopped at six o'clock. He turned off the camcorder, removed the video tape cassette, and hurried into the living room where his mother was waiting. He gave her the cassette, and he and Susie settled in front of the TV set. His mother inserted the cassette into the VCR and rewound it. Then she started the playback and sat on the sofa to see what would happen.

For what seemed forever, the video tape played back and the TV screen showed the computer flashing the time and date on its screen and the cuckoo clock's pendulum swinging back and forth. Unable to wait, Little Bill used the VCR's remote control to increase the volume, and then he used the fast forward setting to advance the tape until the clock read about one minute before six. They watched with anticipation while the clock ticked steadily. Then, at about 15 seconds before the hour, the clock sounded a small series of clicks that Little Bill knew was the cuckoo mechanism preparing to chirp out the hour. At the same time they saw a small blur at the bottom of the screen just below the computer. It was out of sight before they could tell what it was. At exactly six o'clock, the cuckoo's door opened, and the tiny wooden bird came out on a platform to begin chirping. Its beak opened and closed and its body bobbed up and down as the two small bellows in the body of the clock sounded the two syllables of the cuckoo bird's call.

Then they saw it. A small blurred body leapt from the floor to the top of the computer's video monitor. From there it jumped at the clock, barely reaching the pendulum but striking it enough to stop the pendulum in its travel. When the furry white blur landed back on the top of the video monitor, it stopped. Bill and his mother watched first in amazement and then with great glee as they watched Susie's image gingerly step from the video monitor to the computer keyboard and then jump to the floor. Little Bill rewound the tape and reran the sequence in slow motion freezing the frame at the place where Susie stepped on the computer keyboard. Sure enough, her front paw touched exactly on the place where Little Bill knew the keyboard's Pause key was, the key that told the computer to suspend operation until another key was pressed.

With the mystery solved, Little Bill and his mother sat and laughed for a while. Then, with the house back to normal at last, Little Bill resolved to close the door to his study at dinner time from now on, his mother was relieved that the mystery was solved and her son's meals would be on time again, and Susie purred happily in his lap wondering why everyone was petting and praising her so much.

The Dealer

The corner booth at Denny's was his place of business. He bought and sold cars there. That's not usual, dealing cars from a restaurant, but the overhead was low, zero almost. He didn't have business cards, rent, or a phone bill. The staff all knew him and expected to see him come in every morning. He was a fixture, something that you could count on. He hadn't missed a day since he started doing this.

Not long after he started, he made a deal with the manager for his breakfast and lunch every day for a monthly fee. It was easier that way not having to think about getting a meal. Except that every time there was a new waitress she'd always want to take his order. He didn't want to place an order.

"Just fix me something to eat," he'd say.

"But sir, you need to select something from the menu. How'll I know what you want?"

"Look, when my wife was alive, did she hand me a menu every morning, noon, and night? No. She fixed me something to eat, and I ate it. You should do the same." His manner was gentle.

The new waitress would go see the manager, and he'd set her straight. Another one broken in, Joe would say to himself. After a while, she'd take him for granted and treat him like everyone else did. They always liked him after they got to know him. Joe was a nice guy for a used car dealer, that's what everyone said.

The pay phone on the wall inside the alcove to the restrooms was his business line. The back parking lot, seldom used by restaurant customers these days, was his showroom, his lot. He rarely had more than four or five cars. Didn't like to tie his assets up in inventory, he'd say. Regular customers at Denny's knew him. Hi, Joe, they'd call out as they slid into a nearby booth or took a stool at the counter. How's business, they'd want to know. Strangers didn't notice him, just another customer sitting in the corner reading the paper, they thought if they thought anything at all. Then the phone would ring and he'd answer it. That made them wonder.

He ran a standing ad in the local paper. Cash for your car, followed by the number of the pay phone. He ran ads for the cars he had, too. The phone rang a lot.

"Yeah, I advertised the Malibu. How about I meet you at Denny's and you can take it for a spin?"

Or, "You got what? That's twelve years old. It been on the beach? No? How much you want for it? Tell you what, if you'll take less, say four, five hundred, bring it by Denny's on the island. I'll meet you in the corner booth near the back and we'll see."

When calls were slow, Joe browsed the classifieds looking for good cars he could get and sell for a profit. He'd call and talk condition and price, and get the owner to bring it to Denny's for him to look at it. They weren't used to that. Buyers are supposed to come to where the car is.

"If it's cherry like you say, I'll give you your best offer, cash on the line. Bring the title. Better have a ride home lined up in case I take it." They always came.

Joe didn't buy junk. You can't sell junk. He rarely drove the cars they brought by. He could tell by looking if it was in good shape. Best to see tires not new but with even wear. Doesn't smoke or make a lot of noise driving in to meet him. Not too clean, though. He didn't like it if the engine had been detailed or the car had a new paint job. He'd offer them less than they'd get in trade. Most of them didn't want to trade for another car. They needed some cash and they had one more car than they could handle. Motivated sellers, that's what Joe liked. Then he'd sit on the car until he got top dollar.

Selling cars was easy. He'd run them through the car wash and maybe have them waxed. People figured they'd get a better deal from a guy who meets them at Denny's. That wasn't usually the way it happened, but he did have good cars, and plenty of his buyers were repeat trade. A few of them would check in with him to see what he had or ask him to look out for this kind of sedan or that brand of minivan. He usually found what they wanted.

When a buyer he didn't know wanted a test drive, he'd go with them. Teenagers had to show him a driver's license. He didn't get many of them because he stayed away from sports cars or so-called "personal" cars. Four-door sedans, station wagons, minivans, that's what sells.

He used to figure that he lost out on some business when he was out on the lot or on a test drive because he'd miss phone calls. But before he'd been at Denny's for very long, the waitresses started answering the phone and taking messages for him. Jim, the day cook, said he ought to get a cell phone with call forwarding and take it with him outside. He didn't want to do that. You got to keep the overhead down, he'd say. Besides customers didn't like being interrupted while he took another call. It was bad enough while they sat at the booth and dealt or filled out papers.

He used to keep cash on hand to buy cars, but the neighborhood had gone down some in recent years, and so he used a checkbook now. The buyer could go to the bank next door and cash the check, so it wasn't a problem. He accepted only cash though. People he knew could give him a check, but only if he really knew them. Cash sales. Hold no paper. Thirty-thirty guarantee. Thirty feet or thirty seconds.

"Sooner of later they all come through here," he'd say, "I've seen them all." No one knew what he meant when he said that, but he said it a lot.

Once a new manager at Denny's tried to get rid of him. The waitresses all put up a fuss, but the guy held firm. Joe asked what law he was breaking. The guy thought maybe he was loitering or violating his zoning or occupational license or something. That guy was a pain in the ass. Joe didn't figure he was hurting anybody. He held his ground, and the guy cut off his meal deal and threatened to call the cops. Before the guy knew what, one of the county cops stopped in to see about buying a car Joe had on the lot. That stopped the asshole cold. He quit bothering Joe and after a while he moved on. The next guy was better. Joe had a good relationship with the cops. They didn't notice his cars sitting without tags on that rear lot, and he always gave them a good deal on a car.

Every evening he'd pick out a car to drive home with his dealer tag. It didn't matter which one, but if one of the regulars at Mike's had indicated an interest in something like one he had, he'd drive it. Everybody wanted him to get them a car. They thought he'd give them a better deal.

He always stopped at Mike's for a cold one. Ethel hadn't liked that so he only stopped on Fridays when she was still alive. Now he stopped every evening. He had gained some weight, probably from the big breakfasts and lunches that the girls brought him every day. The cold ones helped too. Ethel had always cooked a balanced meal, wanted him to eat lots of fiber and things that were good for him. She got him to quit smoking, and that was a help. The law prohibited smoking in restaurants. He alwars had to go outside to smoke.

Ethel was good for him, the best part of his life. He'd retired with thirty years in the Air Force, a line mechanic, and they moved here to be near the warm weather and the beach. They'd been stationed here in the fifties when he was first in service, and they liked the area. She always wanted to come back. They bought a small house, settled in for a quiet retirement, and six months later she died. He sat around the house for another six months not doing much of anything. He was fifty-three. He mowed the grass when he couldn't stand it any more, and he ate out, usually at Denny's, which was just a mile from his house.

He sold Ethel's car to a guy at Denny's, a regular customer who had one to trade. To help the guy out, he took the trade-in. Then he had to sell the trade-in. That was easy, and so he just started buying and selling cars at Denny's. It was something to do, it got him out of the house, and he met people.

One thing Joe didn't want was another woman. He couldn't see it. It wasn't something he'd talk about, either. He said it to himself once in a while. I had the best. It'd be hard to match what I had much less beat it. But he didn't discuss it with anyone else. Not that he lacked opportunity. Plenty of available ladies in this town what with the divorce rate and all. Nice ones, too. They'd talk to him at Mike's. He could tell they were interested. He couldn't get going though. Nothing wrong with him, he just couldn't get over Ethel that fast. It'd only been a couple years now. But they'd talk to him, invite him to dinner, they wanted to cook for him. He didn't need it.

One day a guy comes in to Denny's and wants Joe to go in partners with him. The government is auctioning off cars like they do every now and then, and the guy wants to get a limousine that they have on the block this time. The government always had exotic cars that they took away from drug dealers. After a while they'd auction them. The guy figures that the limo will go for a steal because nobody wants a limo. The guy doesn't have much money but he figures that with a limo, a black suit, and a cap, he can run a chauffeur service around the beach where the rich tourists hang out. The city cops at the beach had been nailing a lot of drunk drivers, and the snow birds and tourists were afraid to go out. This guy figures they'll pop for a classy ride to and from a bar, a ride that comes with a fresh rose and a bottle of champagne. No cops can bother them that way. He already has the suit and the cap. Only he has no money to get the limo. The guy's name was Charlie. Joe knew him from around town, and nobody ever said anything bad about him, so Joe figured he was probably OK.

Joe liked the idea. and the two of them went to the auction. The limo was in good shape, a stretch Cadillac, silver with gold trim. It had a car phone, wet bar, TV, stereo, even a DVD. The mileage was low and the tires were good. Joe started it up and it purred. Charlie kept yapping about what a great deal it was and how they were going to make a pile running a limo service. Joe told him to shut up. The auctioneer started the bidding at $10,000, which was probably a bargain. Joe figured they might as well go home. No way he'd pay ten grand for any heap. Nobody bid. The auctioneer dropped to eight. Nothing. Six. Nobody budged. The auctioneer asked for any bid. Joe bid fifteen hundred bucks. When nobody else bid anything, the auctioneer brought the gavel down, and Joe bought himself a limo.

The next couple of weeks found Joe setting up a more traditional business than what he had been running. He had cards made up to put in all the hotel lobbies and took out ads in a couple of little throwaway entertainment magazines. He had the car phone activated and got an answering service to take most of the calls when and if they started coming in. He got a listing in the Yellow Pages. The insurance was steep, more for a year than he paid for the car. He made it clear to Charlie that if he wanted to be a partner he'd have to come up with some of the dough. Otherwise he could be a commissioned employee. Charlie took the latter option because he had no dough. He had to keep his suit clean and wash and wax the car. He had to answer the car phone if anyone called. And he had to take Joe to Mike's sometimes and pick him up after an hour or two. Unless there was a real booking for the limo, that is. Business comes first.

It didn't take long before the limo was booked solid on weekends. Joe was surprised at the clientelle they got. A lot of his bookings were from locals who wanted to impress a woman or who were going out on a special occasion like an anniversary or something. There were a lot of retired people in this town. The gold trim made the limo a natural for golden anniversaries. In less than four months the business was in the black. Charlie was happy, and Joe had something else besides the used car racket to keep his mind alive.

One week they told him at Denny's that Saturday would be Annie's birthday. She was going to be 48. Annie was the most recent addition to the crew of waitresses. She'd only been there about two months. She and Joe got along OK but she worked the counter, and he didn't get to talk to her much. Annie was a looker. The guys would come in and flirt with her until they caught her drift. She was all business, friendly enough but not one of those toss-arounds who falls all over every guy just to show herself she's still got it. Annie had class. Joe wasn't sure what class was, but if anyone had it, she did. She had a grown daughter she lived with who worked for the government or one of the contractors at the base, Joe didn't know which. Annie didn't have a steady boyfriend, but she could've if she'd wanted one. Most guys would be proud to have her on their arm.

The other waitresses were all fond of Annie. They wanted to do something for her birthday, and they were talking it up whenever she wasn't there. One of them suggested that they all kick in and rent Joe's limo for Annie for the evening. Joe got wind of it and let them know that the ride would be on the house. He always went out of his way to help the ladies at Denny's. Then they wanted to find her a date, an escort. Joe couldn't help there, he said. But he could tell they were plotting something because whenever two or more of them weren't busy, they'd be in a corner whispering and stealing glances at Joe.

"Look," he told them when they approached him, "it wouldn't be the same. I'm just a guy who sells cars from the corner booth. It's nobody she doesn't already know. It wouldn't be somebody special like you want for her. Besides, how do you know she'd go? Annie can do a lot better than me, and I'm not interested anyway."

"Come on, Joe," Sheila said. "You're perfect. We want her to have dinner and a night out on us with somebody we trust. You're the same age. She must like you, she don't ever say anything against you."

"I don't go out with women, yet. It wouldn't be right."

"It ain't like it's a goddamn date, Joe. You don't have to marry her or nothing. Just two friends on an evening out. Nobody's asking you to go steady or have kids, fer Chrissakes." Sheila could get right to the point. "Besides, there's nobody else we would trust with her. We don't want her to have a bad time on her birthday fighting off some bozo putting a heavy hit on her when she don't know him and don't want it."

Pretty soon they were all leaning on him, pleading and begging the way only a bunch of nice women can do. A guy'd have to be a real jerk to say no to a bunch like that. He gave in, but only if they did the asking first. It was one thing to break his streak of solitude. He was damned if he'd be turned down doing it.

Annie said yes. They told Joe that she was moved that they cared enough to want her to have a nice birthday and that she thought Joe would be a nice escort. The rest of the week she didn't talk to him much, but he'd catch her looking his way from time to time. She'd smile when he caught her, but she didn't come over to talk. Neither did Joe.

He picked her up on Saturday night in the limo. He told Charlie beforehand to act professional, not get chummy with him or anything after they picked her up. Charlie ragged him all the way over there though. He talked about getting a curtain installed on the glass separator between the driver and passenger compartments so Joe and his "fox" could get some privacy. Joe took it for a while then told Charlie to clam up. You always had to tell Charlie to clam up. Otherwise he'd go on for hours.

Annie was impressed with the limo. They talked about nothing in particular during the ride to the restaurant and drank some of the champagne. Charlie kept his lip buttoned, but Joe caught him peeking at them in the mirror a few times. Charlie was right. That curtain would be a good idea. Annie went through the CDs and put one on the stereo. Chuck Berry. Joe would've guessed she was a classical fan. Or maybe Mantovani. You never can tell. The Chuck Berry was his favorite. "Nadine, is that you..."

Dinner at the Santa Fe was nice. The girls had made the arrangements and told Joe what the limit was. They had already given the money to the management. Fifty bucks. Joe had to laugh when he saw the menu. The fifty would just about cover it if you didn't have anything to drink or any coffee after dinner and if you picked the least expensive entrees and didn't tip. The management brought a small birthday cake with one candle for Annie. Joe ignored the fifty dollar limit and paid the difference with a good tip. Annie didn't seem to notice. Joe was enjoying himself in a different way than he had for a long time.

She cleaned up nice, that was for sure. If she was a looker at the counter in her waitress uniform, she was a knockout in her Sunday best. The other men in the restaurant stared when they came in. Joe suspected that Charlie's silence during the ride was more in awe for Annie and her makeup and gown than out of respect for Joe's admonitions to keep still.

They went to Mike's for a drink after dinner. They took a table instead of sitting at the bar like Joe always did. Mike came out from behind the bar and served them, something he never did for anyone. The young girl in the black tuxedo uniform with short shorts and net stockings came in selling roses. They cruised all the bars on weekends looking for couples. You were supposed to feel like a cheapskate if you said no when they pitched, "Buy a rose for the lady, sir?". Joe bought one for Annie.

He let her do the talking. He was glad that she didn't talk about her ex-husband the way the other women at the bar always did. Joe had a joke that he told when people asked why he didn't go out. He said he was looking for the perfect date. When they bit and asked what the perfect date was, Joe told them it was someone who didn't talk about her divorce, didn't talk about winning the lottery, and didn't snore. Annie was at least two out of three. She talked about her childhood, her parents and brothers and the small town she grew up in. She liked to read and told him about the book she was reading. She liked mysteries and didn't like romance novels. Joe didn't read much except for automative magazines and the newspaper.

They left Mike's and Joe told Charlie to drive south past the Air Force base to where cars parked during the day to go to the beach. There was a wooden walkway from the parking area to the beach, and Joe and Annie sat on one of the wooden benches. She held the rose in both hands and watched the reflection of the moon in the ocean. Luck would have it, the moon was a day or two shy of being full and the tide was out. It was quiet and peaceful. They brought the last of the champagne with them. Annie talked some more, about where she grew up, about her daughter, about a cruise she took just before she came to work at Denny's. Joe wondered why a classy dame like Annie worked at Denny's. It's all there is, she told him. She had no skills, couldn't even type. She'd spent her life being a housewife and raising a son and daughter. The only mention she made of her ex was to say that he'd been good to her after the divorce while the kids were growing up and in college. He saw to it that she lived well enough that they had a good home. When they went to college, he picked up their support, and she had to go to work to take care of herself. She sold the house and got the apartment. The proceeds from the house made a nice retirement nest egg. The job paid her keep. With her daughter living with her now and sharing expenses, the way was easier. She wasn't exactly Princess Di, but she wasn't starving either.

The champagne was gone and Charlie would be wanting to get home. Joe and Annie left the beach, and they had to wake Charlie up. When they dropped Annie off, Joe went to the door with her. She took his hand and thanked him for a nice evening. She'd ask him in but her daughter would be getting ready for bed now. That's OK, Charlie needs to get home. They stood awkwardly for a moment and then Joe took his hand back and said goodnight and walked back to the limo. Charlie was asleep again. Joe got in the back and sat for a while. The touch of her hand and the warmth of her parting smile stayed with him. He felt good. He put the Chuck Berry CD on again, leaned back and looked out the smoked glass past the apartment building at the moon above some palm trees. Chuck Berry's music filled the night.

"Oh, Carol, don't let him steal it away...."

ELIZA-911

At 12:02 on Saturday morning the 911 emergency phone rang at the Devlin County Sheriff's Office. Belinda Stark stubbed out her first cigarette of the evening and typed the call-answer command into the new ELIZA-911 emergency console keyboard. ELIZA's 10-inch voice recorder reels began their slow rotation, and the address and phone number of the caller popped up on the video screen:

Belinda made a mental note of the address. Stillwater Road is the only road down an eight-mile peninsula that divides the Back River and Stillwater Creek. The 2800 block is near the tip of the peninsula, and she knew that if the caller needed personal attention, a deputy would have to drive the eight miles to the end where expensive waterfront homes with indoor pools and covered docks were tucked away in thick palmetto and palm clusters. She spoke into the tiny transmitter mounted on the thin tube that sloped down from the earpiece of her headset.

"Sheriff's Office."

The man's voice on the other end had that rushed urgency often heard in a 911 caller, but he spoke in a hoarse whisper.

"This is Peter Morse. I think someone has broken into my house."

"Are you there now, sir?" she asked.

"Yes. I'm in the garage on an extension phone. I just went down to the Fast Market for cigarettes, and when I got back, I called you. You'd better send somebody quick."

"Is your address 2804 Stillwater Road?" The ELIZA-911 system and the hookup with the phone company's digital switch were new, and Belinda neither understood nor trusted them. She always asked callers to verify what ELIZA's screen displayed.

"Yes, of course. How did you know?"

"You said you think someone broke in. Aren't you sure?"

"I haven't gone in yet, but a light is on that was off when I left, and I heard a noise coming from inside when I got out of my car. It sounded like something falling or breaking. I think they're still in there."

That last part snapped Belinda to attention. A burglary is in progress, and the occupant is on the premises. Belinda abandoned her usual slow drawl and spoke quickly.

"Sir, listen very carefully. A deputy will be there as soon as possible. Don't go inside until he gets there, do you understand? Do not go in the house. Leave the garage if you can and go to a neighbor's house to wait."

"No, I'll wait here. Just get somebody down here quick. I've got a lot of valuable stuff."

"Yes sir. Is any other member of your family at home?"

"No, I live alone."

"All right, if you don't want to go to a neighbor's house, stay on the line with me until the deputy gets there."

Her words were cut off. Peter Morse had hung up. Belinda typed the dispatch command. ELIZA hung up the phone and switched the microphone to the police band radio transmitter. Belinda sent out a call asking for the patrol car nearest Stillwater Road. She used the staccato police jargon that substitutes numbers and phrases for what's really happening.

"Robbery in progress at 2804 Stillwater. Occupant on or near premises. Code 3."

Deputy Fred Baldwin was only a half mile from where the Devlin Beach Causeway turns onto Stillwater. He answered the call with a terse, "Car 22 responding, just near the Pontiac dealer."

After Fred's response, Belinda pressed ELIZA's dispatch-complete function key. A small computer printer clacked out a printed log that showed the times and activities related to the call. The 10-inch tape rewound itself to the beginning of the call and copied the phone call and radio dispatch onto a microcassette. It stopped just past the recorded conversations. Belinda tore the log from the continuous-form perforated paper and replaced the microcassette with a blank. ELIZA was ready for the next 911 call. Belinda put the log and microcassette into a manilla jacket, clasped and labeled it, and lit her second cigarette of the evening.

Sheriff Simon Tate woke from a deep sleep. It took several seconds to realize that the ringing in his dream came from the phone on the night stand. He fumbled around the night stand until he found the offending instrument and pulled it to his ear. Out of habit he made a mental note of the time glowing on the digital clock radio next to the phone. 12:43 AM.

"Sheriff Tate."

"Simon, this is Belinda. Fred has a homicide down at the end of Stillwater. He needs you to come down there. I've already called the Medical Examiner's Office."

Tate shook the cobwebs from his brain. "Right. On my way, Belinda. Call those guys back and tell them not to touch anything until I get there. How'd Fred get onto it?"

"He answered a nine-eleven call for a burglary."

"Who called it in?"

"A Peter Morse. Fred thinks Morse is the victim."

Sheriff Tate hung up the phone and looked around for his trousers. He was in his fifties, balding and slightly overweight. He had come to Devlin county after his retirement from an undistinguished and unflawed career as a State Police investigator. He was a calm and intelligent man who avoided aclaim simply because nothing much ever happened on his beat. He had an uncomplicated and routine police job and liked for things to stay that way. Murders were not the way to keep things simple. He finished dressing and went outside to his car.

Driving to the Stillwater turnoff, Tate pondered the stupidity of Devlin County crooks. Why would anyone break into a house at the end of an eight-mile, one-road peninsula? That's where the rich people live, but a burglar's chances of success are slim. The only getaway route is that eight-mile stretch with no turnoffs. If somebody sees the robbery, the cops have plenty of time to get a roadblock up while the robber is trying to get away. A boat wouldn't work either because the water is too shallow. Tate turned right onto Stillwater and headed south. Eight miles later he arrived at the crime scene.

Peter Morse's was one of the smaller houses on Stillwater Road. Sheriff Tate pulled up next to Fred's patrol car and noted that the garage door was raised. A sedan was parked inside with the driver's door standing open. The flashing blue lights on the patrol car had attracted the attention of the neighborhood, and several robe-clad neighbors were milling around in the narrow road in front of the house. They were passing around a thermos of coffee and talking quietly among themselves. Most of the houses were lit up suggesting that those who weren't part of the curious gathering were out of bed and waiting to see what had happened. A black Ford displaying the County Medical Examiner's emblem pulled into the driveway. A sleepy assistant medical examiner got out of the car and joined Tate. They exchanged nods and went into the house.

Fred Baldwin was in the foyer taking pictures. The house was a shambles. Furniture was overturned, pictures were crooked or off the wall, drawers were pulled out. The many possessions of a man who lived alone were strewn everywhere.

"Where's the deceased?" asked the medical examiner.

"In the shower off the master bedroom. Down the hall to the right."

"He was taking a shower?" Tate was surprised.

"No. He's fully dressed."

"What's the rest of the house like?"

"There's an office over the garage. It's all torn up too. It's not vandalism, though. Nothing's destroyed or damaged, but the books and papers are all over the floor."

"Have you talked to the neighbors yet?"

"A few stuck their heads in. None of them heard or saw anything," said Fred.

Fred told the sheriff that he had answered the call from Belinda and rushed to the scene with siren and lights going. The garage and front doors were wide open, and the outside light was on. He entered the house with his revolver drawn and found the mess. During his search he found the body in the shower. No one else was on the premises. The body was still warm, and it had what looked like a bullet wound in the right temple.

"Did you call for an ambulance?" asked Tate.

"No, the guy was dead, no doubt about that. I called Belinda."

"While you were tearing down Stillwater did you see any cars going out?"

"Nobody passed me."

The assistant medical examiner came back into the foyer. "One bullet wound in the right temple from close up. He died instantly and has been dead about two hours. Time of death is between midnight and twelve-thirty. There's a pistol on the floor by the bathroom door. Let me know when we can take the remains. I'll call for the wagon now."

"Thanks," said Tate as the examiner went out to radio from his car. Tate went down the hall and into the master bedroom. The bed was made, but nothing else in the room seemed in its proper order. Clothes were everywhere, bureau drawers were thrown on the floor, a video cassette recorder was knocked off its stand and its cassettes were scattered about. The TV was rolled away from the wall, and its cable connection was torn loose. The bathroom was to the left and its door was open into the bathroom. Towels, soap, and men's toilet articles were all over the vanity and floor, and a large athletic supporter dangled from the doorknob. Tate wondered whether this guy was a slob or the burglar liked throwing laundry around.

A revolver was on the floor by the bathroom door. Tate picked it up by pushing a pencil into its barrel. From the way the pencil went all the way into the chamber, Tate could tell that the bullet in the firing position had been expended. He took a plastic zip-lock sandwich bag from his pocket and dropped the gun into it. Then he sealed the bag and put it back on the floor where he had found the gun.

The shower stall entrance was six feet into the bathroom past the double sink vanity and the toilet, and the body was slumped on the tile floor in the shower. A shower curtain hung loosely from its hooks on a rod across the arched entrance to the shower. The curtain was crumpled at eye level and had a scorched hole just above the wrinkled place. Tate pulled out a red evidence tag and tagged the shower curtain. Despite the slick tile floor, Tate managed to chalk the position of the body. The medical examiner would want to move it soon.

Fred came into the bedroom. He poked his head into the bathroom and said, “Need anything more from me, Sheriff?”

“Yeah,” said Tate. “Bag up this shower curtain and all these clothes and get them and the gun to the lab first thing in the morning. Tell the lab guys to dust the whole house for prints. Make an inventory of everything in the house. Maybe we can figure out what’s missing from what’s left. Prepare a statement for the press telling what we know, nothing more or less. I’m going home.”

Sheriff Tate was at the office early the next morning. He was bleary-eyed from lack of sleep and not too happy about being there. Saturday was his day off, and he didn’t like giving it up. Belinda was just turning the shift over to Jenny, the day dispatcher, and she came into Tate’s office.

“Here’s ELIZA’s log and tape for the Stillwater case. I thought you’d want it first thing.”

“Thanks, Belinda. Have Fred check with me before he signs out.”

“Fred already went home. He sent the shower curtain and pistol to the State Police lab for tests. The inventory of the house’s contents is on your desk. You’ll have all the pictures this afternoon. The coroner isn’t in yet, but you should have his report by sometime this afternoon, too.”

“Thanks. I’ll be on Stillwater Peninsula the rest of the morning talking to Morse’s neighbors. Tell Jenny to take messages until I get back. Have we heard from the press?”

“I gave them the statement first thing this morning. Here’s a copy. Peter Morse was a minor national celebrity, a writer. He wrote movie and TV scripts for mystery shows. A reporter from California already called here this morning.”

An hour later, Simon Tate sat in the private office over Peter Morse’s garage. The office was comfortable. Large picture windows on three sides offered views of the river to the east, Stillwater Creek to the west and the peninsula to the north. Out the east window he could see the police barricade at the driveway entrance. Occasionally a Channel 6 News van drove by.

Talks with the neighbors hadn’t yielded much. Stillwater peninsula was one of those communities where people knew who their neighbors were but generally did not know one another. If they socialized, it was through some outside organization such as a local church, country club or health spa. Peter Morse belonged to no such groups according to the neighbors. Because of his status as a minor celebrity, everyone on Stillwater Road knew who he was, but few knew him. Most of them saw him only when he drove in and out. Perhaps that was why he ignored Belinda's advice to wait with a neighbor until the police got there.

Only one family seemed to have known Morse. They often had Morse to dinner. Morse must have liked them because he usually accepted their invitations. They thought he had no other friends. He would pay for his dinner by entertaining them with stories of his celebrity aquaintances. In the last two years he would talk vaguely about different unfinished projects, but the neighbors had not seen his name in the TV credits for a long time. They always looked for it. Morse had been evasive when they first mentioned it, so they avoided the subject after that. They said Morse seemed troubled the last several weeks. He had mentioned a new television project, a non-fictional expose of sorts, and had talked about some sinister element that might be associated with the project. He had declined to give them any details, saying the less the neighbors knew, the safer they would be. Someone might use extreme measures to suppress the project, he said.

The southern wall of Morse's office was lined with bookcases, each of them filled with books and magazines. Two filing cabinets sat at one end of the south wall and a desk was in the middle of the room. In front of the filing cabinets were stacks of files and papers where the deputies had left them after they cleaned up. Behind the desk was a table with a personal computer, a computer printer, and stacks of floppy diskettes. Maybe something in that computer could shed some light on the puzzle that was building around Morse's death. Tate picked up the phone and dialed Fred's home number. Fred had a home computer and spent a lot of time playing with it. Maybe he could make some sense out of all this stuff. Fred's wife answered and said he was out and would be back soon. Tate gave her Morse's phone number and asked her to tell Fred to call as soon as he returned.

Tate hoped that something in the home computer would provide a clue to the mysterious expose project that Morse had mentioned to the neighbors. If Morse was working on something that someone wanted to stifle, the project records might shed some light on his killer. So far the personal papers and files were only contracts, manuscripts, and reference materials for past projects. Everything seemed innocent enough, related to works of fiction, mostly mystery scripts for long-since canceled detective shows. There were no papers that pertained to any writing project newer than two years old. If Morse had any new scripts in the works, Tate couldn't find them.

Morse's bank statements showed that he didn't have much money but he had a steep mortgage payment on the house, payments on the car, and several other outstanding loans. He also had several minor life insurance policies and one recent one with a big payoff. The beneficiary was a women named Martha Powell who lived in a nearby county.

Tate had the ELIZA-911 log and microcassette with him and had gone over them several times. As near as he could tell, Sammy was at the Morse house within twelve minutes from the time Morse dialed 911. The conversation between Morse and Belinda had taken just over one minute. It took fifteen seconds to raise Sammy and another fifteen before Belinda hit the dispatch-complete function key. It would have taken Sammy no more than a minute to get to Stillwater Road from the Pontiac dealer. If he was code three, he probably averaged 40 miles an hour down the winding eight miles of Stillwater Road, putting him at Morse's house in about ten minutes. All together, the response should have taken no more than thirteen minutes. In that time Peter Morse apparently went into the house, found it ransacked, and searched for the burglar. Instead of Morse finding the burglar, the burglar found him, shot him, and then escaped down a narrow road with no turnoffs and a deputy hell-bent-for-leather coming straight at him.

Why did Morse go into the house knowing the police were on the way? Why did the killer leave the gun? Why did the killer shoot him? Was the burglar looking for something specific? Only the living quarters and office were disturbed. The kitchen, garage and pool area were untouched. Tate gathered the papers he wanted and went downstairs to have another look around the garage.

Morse's car was still in the garage. One of the deputies had closed the door. Tate opened it and peered inside. Just then a phone rang. Tate looked around and saw a wall-phone extension by the door into the house. He got out of the car, picked up the phone, and got a dial tone. Then the phone rang again from inside the house. Stepping into the kitchen he found another phone and picked it up. It was Fred returning his call.

"Fred, can you come down to the Morse house and help me find something on Morse's home computer?."

"Sure, I'll be right there."

As soon as Tate hung up the phone rang again. It was Jenny, the day shift dispatcher.

"Sheriff Tate, the lab reports are in on the shower curtain and gun. The gun had no fingerprints but it was the murder weapon. The hole in the shower curtain had powder burns around it."

"What about the house?" asked the sheriff.

"One set of prints, probably belonging to the deceased. We'll verify it after the coroner's report comes in."

"Ok, do me one more favor, Jenny. Find out who Martha Powell is. If she's a relative, we'll have to notify her of Morse's death. If the newspapers haven't already done it, that is." Tate read Martha Powell's address from the insurance policy to Jenny and hung up the phone. He continued to poke around the papers and files while he waited for Fred.

Four hours later Fred turned off Peter Morse's personal computer and swung around in the swivel chair. He had been probing the innards of the computer ever since he had arrived. He looked puzzled.

"Sheriff, people like Morse use these things for several different purposes, but mainly as word processors to do their writing. Most of the scripts and manuscripts that you found in his files are recorded here on floppy disks. He used it for his financial records, too. If the tax records I found are correct, Morse owed the IRS a lot of money. His income last year was all from residuals for reruns of stuff he wrote years ago. He made a lot of money in the past, but his residuals have been going down as his stuff goes out of reruns. He owes a bunch of taxes and some pretty stiff penalties.

"The odd part has to do with his writing. The files on the word processor diskettes are all recorded with the date and time they were last updated. Talk about writer's block. If Peter Morse wrote anything in the last two years, he didn't keep it in here."

Tate considered that remark and said, "Or someone took it. Did Morse label his diskettes in a way that would make it easy for someone to know what was on them?"

"No, he's like most home computer users. His diskettes are scattered in random stacks with mostly cryptic labels, and the file names don't really say what's in the files."

"How long would it take an intruder to find what he's looking for in that pile of diskettes?"

"Hours, probably. He'd need to look at every disk file. Even that isn't so simple. He'd need to know what software to use for each disk. You look at the word processing stuff with the word processor program; the data base files need the data base manager program; the financial records need the spreadsheet program. Your intruder would have to be a better computer hacker than me to be able to sift through this mess in anything less than the time I've taken."

Back in his office Simon Tate reviewed the pile of material he had accumulated on the life and death of Peter Morse. The photos of the crime scene had been developed and delivered, and the ballistics and coroner's reports were in. The revolver was the murder weapon. No record of the gun was on file. It was an old model from before gun registration was required. Tate requested an FBI trace of the serial number but held little hope that anything would turn up. The fingerprints in the house all belonged to Morse.

Martha Powell was Morse's daughter, married and living at the address shown on the insurance policy. When Simon called her, she said that Morse's neighbors had already notified her. She was coming to Devlin County as soon as possible to make arrangements. She knew nothing of the insurance policy or any of Morse's other affairs. They had not been in touch recently. Morse's wife had been dead for several years.

Fred had followed Tate back to the station from the Morse house. He was sitting across from the sheriff waiting to see what would happen next.

"Fred, let's review what we have on this murder. We've got a has-been mystery writer who lives alone. Apparently he hasn't worked lately, and he's in debt to the eyes. He seems to have lost touch with reality, talking about mysterious expose projects and sinister plots. We can't find a trace of any such work. No contract, no notes, no manuscript, nothing."

"Maybe the killer got it."

"He didn't have time. Morse said he just went out for cigarettes. You yourself said it would have taken the killer hours to find any evidence of an expose in Morse's records. No, I don't think any killer was looking for any mythical expose."

"Simple burglary?"

"Look at this inventory. A TV, A VCR, antiques, a stereo, some diamond cuff links, a lot of other stuff that a burglar would have taken."

"But the burglar was surprised by Morse. Maybe he left without taking anything."

"Let's look at the time element. Morse probably wasn't gone much more than half an hour. The killer had that much time to break in and tear up the house, then about ten more minutes to hide from Morse, wait for Morse to peek into the shower, kill him, and leave before you got there. What was Morse doing in the shower stall, fully clothed, with the curtain drawn?"

"Hiding, maybe. Looking for the intruder. How about a hired killer? He waits for Morse to get in the shower and uses the curtain to muffle the shot."

"That plastic curtain wouldn't muffle a mouse sneeze. Why would a professional killer wait for Morse to hide in the shower? He could've just popped Morse when he walked in from the garage. Surely he wasn't afraid of a skinny old guy like Morse."

"Well, Sheriff, you've ruled out every possibility. It's either murder or suicide. It couldn't have been suicide because of where we found the gun. You don't shoot yourself and then throw the gun across the room. That leaves murder, maybe a robbery, but nothing was taken. Sounds to me like a hit that was intentionally made to look like a robbery."

"Let's pursue that from a different angle. Suppose it was neither murder nor robbery but was made to look like both. Morse said on the phone that he was calling from the garage, didn't he?"

"Yeah, so what?"

"Well, the only phone number we have is the one that shows up on the ELIZA-911 system log."

"So?"

"So, this morning I gave that number to your wife. You called me back on it. When you did, the phone in the garage didn't ring, and when I picked it up, I got a dial tone. You were calling me on the phone in the house. Later the office called on the same line—the one in the house, not the garage. Morse has two phone lines, and the one in the garage is not the one he called 911 with. Remember, Morse as much as told us he didn't know about the new ELIZA-911 system. He asked how Belinda knew his address. He made that call from inside the house and wanted us to believe it came from the garage."

"Why?"

"So his suicide would look like a murder and his new insurance policy would pay off. Most insurance policies don't cover suicide until the policy is two years old. Morse was in financial trouble. Everything he owned would've gone to his creditors. His daughter would've gotten nothing."

"Suicide? What about the gun? We found it six feet away from the body!"

"I think I might have that one figured out, too. Did we find any workout clothes, gym shorts, running shoes, or anything like that among Morse's stuff?"

"No."

"And the neighbors said he wasn't a member of any health spa, so he wouldn't have that stuff in a locker somewhere. You saw the body, what size would you say Morse was?"

"Small. Skinny, actually."

"Right. A little old guy who never works out. So how do you explain that oversized jock strap hanging from his bathroom doorknob?"

That night Belinda Stark pulled her chair up to the dispatcher's desk and picked up the evening paper. She read the story of Peter Morse, a failed man so desperate that he took his own life, faking a robbery-murder so his insurance would clean the slate and leave something for his only survivor, his daughter. The story reported Sheriff Simon Tate's theory of how Morse, a once-renowned mystery writer, had used his creative ingenuity to contrive the near-perfect hoax.

First he set the scene by fabricating a mysterious project that sinister forces might attempt to suppress. Then, on the evening of the crime, Peter Morse scattered his belongings around the house to make it look like an intruder was searching for something. He called the police on the 911 emergency number, saying that he had come home and found a burglary in progress. Then he took his unregistered revolver into the bathroom. He wrapped one side of an oversized athletic supporter around the bathroom doorknob, looped the other side around the handle of the revolver, and twisted the supporter. He got into the shower, stretching the supporter across the room, and gripped the revolver through the shower curtain pointing the barrel at his head. When he pulled the trigger, he was killed instantly, and his hand released the gun. Just as he had planned and probably practices, the supporter yanked the gun from his hand and jerked it across the room, dropping it next to the door. The supporter untwisted itself then and dangled from the doorknob.

Peter Morse planned the perfect suicide down to the last detail, but he failed to consider the one element that could ruin his scheme. He did not consider it because he did not know about ELIZA-911.

Belinda smiled at the silent console with its tape reels, keyboard, and video monitor as ELIZA and Belinda waited for the next 911 caller. She tossed the paper on the desk, leaned back, and lit her first cigarette of the evening.

It

Janie left on Sunday to be away and think it over. There had been another argument, leaving them both with the usual hollow feeling. The fight, like all their fights, had no point, and neither of them would have claimed a victory, just another round fought to a draw. They both wished they didn't set one another off so, and both looked for new ways to make peace and start over, but any discussion meant to make amends usually wound up in another minor skirmish.

Ned knew he had added a brick to the wall that was growing between him and Janie. He couldn't help himself. Whenever she made the simplest of casual observations, no matter how trivial, he felt compelled to correct her, to revise her view of things in which he was expert, to share his knowledge, to maintain his position as the authority on anything, everything, whatever subject was at hand. Of course, she always reacted. The original point stopped being the issue, and her right to hold an opinion took over. He knew this about himself and had tried many times to change. He never realized he was doing it until it was too late. She would go off crying in the bedroom and he would retreat to his study to brood with remorse.

Their fights were never mean. Unlike other couples, neither of them resorted to spiteful cheap shots meant only to hurt. Instead, their arguments were civil and rational debates, meaningful exchanges, without passion or apparent anger. He would offer unwanted criticisms of her ideas, her opinions, or her motives, and she would react defensively. She could think of no real reason to be mad at him. He could not be mad at her. Their logic told them that there was no malice in their attitudes toward one another. Even so, he hurt her again, and now she was gone, telling him as she left that she had to decide whether she could stay with him any more. She had gone away a few times before but never with those words.

She took the good car, his car, leaving him with the old one, her car. That was all right, he supposed. She would be driving the three hours to her parents' house, the pretense being that the visit was on a whim. She would be safer in the more reliable car. Nonetheless, he caught himself rehearsing the petty speech that would gently chide her, "Did you have to take my car? I needed it to ..." He caught himself and thought he'd better stop before he got too far into it. As before, she would think it out, miss him, call him, and come home after a couple of days. Things would be as they were until the next time. That's what made it tolerable, those extended periods when they didn't fight and got along the way a couple are supposed to. Then it was nice. It would be like that again.

Ned Caplan tried to understand why he was the way he was. For as long as he could remember, even before they lived together, before they married, he had used his wit and verbal skills to maintain a superior presence. Sometimes when he was in the middle of one of his lectures, as she called them, he was suddenly aware that it was happening again. Something in his past must have instilled such a towering feeling of insecurity that he needed the constant reassurance of a battle won, a higher rung gained, another notch scored. Before they were married she had been impressed with his confidence and authority. He did not realize that she saw them differently now and found herself too often their unwilling object. What she had once seen as his intellectual strength she now thought was little more than overbearing arrogance.

He spent Sunday puttering with small household activities to make time pass and to keep him from thinking about the fight. In a few days she'd return and everything would be normal. He filled the time with one chore after another, always looking to do something that would please her, something she'd notice when she got home. She'd be happy, would hug him as his reward for fixing whatever it was, and everything would be better. They'd forget the fight, and in the moment of the reunion her recent absence would turn into what she had already pretended to her parents it was: a spontaneous visit, nothing wrong, just dropping in. That's how he'd patch it up; he'd please her and make her proud again. She would tell all the news and gossip from back home, they'd sit up late talking, then to bed to make love.

He wished she'd come home today.

Monday was worse. He missed her most in the morning, missed his morning ritual of bringing coffee before she got up and missed watching her get dressed. He could never express the happiness and contentment he felt when he watched her in any small, routine activity. His words of love, when he managed to say them, always seemed stiff and insincere, not reflecting how he felt but seeming instead to have some ulterior purpose, perhaps to get her to do something he wanted her to do, a poorly-acted seduction of sorts. His timing was usually bad, his instincts never telling him the proper time to speak his feelings, his normal matter-of-fact shell disguising the sincerity of the words.

Driving her old car to his office, he wondered if she'd called her job to say she wouldn't be there today. Perhaps he should call and ask for her and ask when she was expected back. No, that wouldn't do. They would know his voice and know something was wrong. It would seem that he was looking for her, and he did not want to give that impression. On the other hand, she might be there. Maybe she came back early or never went up state at all. Where would she have spent the night? With a girl friend? Which one? The friend would know then that there was trouble. He did not want to let others in on his personal problems. No, surely she went to her parents as she said she would.

His work filled the day and made it pass quickly. Occasionally, when he paused and wondered, time dragged, and then it seemed forever since he'd seen her and longer until he'd see her again. The hard part was not knowing where she was and what she was thinking. If he could talk to her, he could say what was necessary to get her thinking on the right track. His apology as she left had been sincere and was meant to keep her from leaving, but it hadn't worked. It worried him that she was thinking and making decisions without his influence and guidance. It would not occur to him that she needed the opportunity to attend to her thoughts without help, particularly his help.

Her parents would sense something was wrong. They were always sensitive to her moods. But they would ask no questions and decline to interfere. That was how they had always been. Good people, her parents, more his family than anyone of his own could have been.

The remote chance that she was not with them kept him from calling to talk to her. That would make them worry and would add to his imaginary growing list of people who knew about their troubles. He did not want the world knowing he had problems at home or, worse, to appear to be calling around looking for his wife as if he had lost track (or control?) of her. He recalled the times he had seen other men in that circumstance and was reminded of his amused and smug inner reaction. He did not want to be thought of that way.

The drive home filled Ned with apprehension. Surely she'd be back, and they would talk. He'd pull into the driveway and see his car in the garage. As he dealt with the traffic and noise, he rehearsed first one scene then another. Each imaginary dialogue fell apart when he got to the part where she spoke; he did not know what she would say and could not guess.

During the drive he made a firm resolution. From now on he would measure his words and his motives before speaking up. He resolved to become a quiet person, one whose opinions were respected because you rarely heard them, and when you did, they had substance. He already knew that his opinions had substance but felt they lacked respect perhaps because there were so many of them. Withhold the unimportant ones and people will want to hear the important ones. Wait even then to be asked. He wondered if he could do it, if he could simply erase a lifetime of compulsive behavior. He wondered how many of his so-called intellectual friends would have the perception to conclude so simple a solution to so complex a problem. He couldn't wait to tell Janie about it.

She wasn't there. The driveway was empty, and there was no sign that she'd been home. The telephone answering machine was silent with no message for him to call her. He sat at the kitchen table and at last quietly wept, missing her terribly and grateful that no one was there to see him.

They had married while they both were still in school. Her parents wanted them to wait, but yielded to their youthful insistence. He had no family of his own except for a distant uncle and some cousins. His mother died in his first year of college. He never knew his father and had no brothers or sisters. He worked summers and devoted the rest of the year to studying. They met in a class and worked on a few lab projects together, becoming close friends. Their times together outside of class were focused on the school and its activities. She was involved in drama and music, and he was a member of several student political groups. He got her interested in the lectures and seminars of his political clubs, and she took him to plays and concerts. They smoked a little pot and with it discovered the vibrant feeling of unique experience together. Eventually, knowing somehow that together they were special, they came naturally to the conclusion that they should share each other for life. In their senior year, they had a small wedding in her home town. After graduation, they moved to a suburb of the state capitol where, as he put it, he began his career and she got a job. They bought a small house and consciously postponed starting a family until the time was right. She preferred an early start but he wanted more security. They had been married now for four years.

His life was happy. She filled his world with home and routine and shared her family with him. Her parents had immediately accepted him as a son, and he was included in all family matters. His job was satisfying, and the rest of his life was stimulating and properly balanced. There was the young men's civic group to occupy his spare time and the house and lawn to take of. She had a small garden and involved them in the community theater and the local symphony. He organized and directed fund-raising projects for worthy causes while she played the piano and painted a little. Their brief college indulgence in pot was behind them and forgotten, replaced by wine at dinner and a rare White Russian or beer at the local pub where friendly people wore tweed jackets and wool sweaters, smoked pipes, listened to modern jazz, and played an occasional game of darts or chess. Together they lived his image of the ideal American dream, what others called Yuppies. Every now and then they argued. Usually she listened to his opinions with respect. Infrequently she flared up at one of them. He never knew which way it would go. Now she was gone.

Supper was a ham sandwich and milk. He never learned to cook because he never needed to. He had gone from his mother's home to college cafeterias to the well-attended kitchen of his wife who had learned well from her mother. He wondered how long Janie would be gone and thought maybe he should consider what a life alone would be like. He began taking mental inventory of clean laundry and groceries. He could handle the laundry, assuming the machines and detergents hadn't changed much since school and the laundromat. Shopping for meals would be another matter. So would their preparation. He envisioned a lot of meals at fast food restaurants. It occurred to him that he did not know what bills to pay or where she kept the checkbooks and financial records. He briefly enjoyed wondering what it would be like to date again. Enough of this speculation, he thought, better take the more positive attitude that she'll be back soon. How he wished he could talk to her.

After supper came the long hours until bedtime. He needed to fill the space with something to occupy his mind. When she was there, he would watch some TV or read, never paying much attention to her presence but mindful of it, nonetheless. He knew that TV or a book could not fill the void that her absence created. He tried to think of some other chore to be done around the house, something she'd asked him to do. As it did yesterday, the idea of doing something to please her gave him comfort and helped him to believe that she'd return soon, and the storm would be over. He couldn't think of anything else. All the little jobs were done, finished yesterday. He turned on the cable news channel and watched until they began repeating their news stories. It would be eleven o'clock soon, the telephone evening rates would be in effect, and he could settle down at their personal computer and log onto online services to keep busy, to keep his mind off of her. He'd stay up all night if he had to.

Maybe a sleeping pill. She had an Ambian prescription for when she had trouble dozing off. He went to the medicine chest in the bathroom, found the pills and took one from the vial. He was about to return the vial when a blank spot in the cabinet caught his attention.

It wasn't there. He noticed that it was missing. It was gone. It was always there except when they used it. It always stayed in the same place—bottom shelf, left side. Why wasn't it there now? For almost an hour, he searched the bathroom and bedroom, looking everywhere that it could be. It was unthinkable that with her sense of order, she would have put it anywhere other than in its proper place. Yet, he was always the one who got it out so that they would use it, and she was always the one to put it away when they were done. With an empty and cold numbness he said the words to himself that he did not want to believe.

"She must have taken it with her."

He went downstairs into the kitchen,and made a strong drink. He sat for a while in the dark kitchen next to the telephone. He had to call her. It was midnight when he finished his second drink and dialed her parents' number. A sleepy mother-in-law answered the phone. "Mom, it's Ned. Is Janie there?"

"Why no, she isn't." his mother-in-law said.

His stomach sank to his knees. She didn't go to her parents; she went somewhere else. His face felt ice cold. He had to ask, probably spilling the beans.

"She got there OK, didn't she?"

"Oh, yes, yesterday, but she went out earlier this evening. I don't know when she'll be back. Is anything wrong? Should she call you?"

No, she needn't call. He'd talk to her later, sorry to bother them.

Now, what to think? Janie went where she said, but now she was out in her home town where she had grown up, grown into a woman well before they met, out where she had friends from a time before him, old boy friends, now men, and she had taken it with her. He tried to think. How often had she gone home without him? How recently? Odd that he could not remember, that the significance of those other visits escaped him until now. He wondered why he'd never noticed the empty spot in the medicine chest during those other visits. He guessed he'd just never looked. There was a dull, steady ache in the pit of his stomach, an ache he'd never felt before. Maybe it would go away if he could sleep.

Another drink would help.

Sleep would not come, and the alcohol deepened his depression and magnified the imagined importance of all that had happened. When had he lost her? What pivotal event turned her away from him? He could not know, could not guess. In his mind he saw her in situations that made him scared, angry, and resentful—saw her using it with someone else. His imagination kept him awake until the exhaustion of his emotions wore him down, and he slept at last.

Janey pulled the BMW off the interstate onto the exit ramp and turned in the direction toward her job. She decided to go to work instead of going home first. She'd missed one day and didn't want to lose more time. Not only would the work be piling up, but her absences would use her vacation time.

The trip to her parents' had been a welcome relief from the tensions that had been building between Ned and her. Her parents were curious but asked nothing, respecting her privacy. Her mother had said simply that they were there if Janey needed them and left it at that. She spent most of her time in her room or at the lake. Last night she went out and Ned had called. She had sat alone in the small bar where they'd spent so much time while they were dating. From the booth they always shared she hoped to organize her thoughts and decide what to do next. After several hours she decided that she'd go back and make him sit quietly long enough for her to say what she thought was wrong. If he insisted on downplaying the importance of her concerns or—worse yet—pretending that they did not exist, then she would leave him. If he agreed that changes were needed and possible, she would stay while they tried to work it out together. For once, he had to shut up and listen—listen with an open mind. If it was possible for him to do that.

She worked hard to catch up from the missed day and left early to get home before he did. At home, she roamed the house to assess how much having this house meant to her and whether she could give it up. Her feelings were divided between her care for Ned and their marriage and her proprietary concern for her own self-esteem and well-being. She had no of knowing what would happen next.

Several months later Ned sat at his desk in the study and stared out the window. The leaves on the trees in the back yard were at the end of their fall change and had fallen. By now he would have had them raked. This year it did not seem to matter. The yard was in the same neglected condition as the house. Ned had been home from court just an hour. The divorce ritual took just a few minutes.

He and Janie had not spoken. They had agreed in a civil and adult manner to divide everything evenly. He kept the house because he must stay in the town to keep his job. They would continue to own it together and he would make the payments. She took the furniture and household items that she needed, leaving him what he needed. Their divorce was like their marriage—orderly, civilized, with willing concessions, without malice or outward emotion.

He remembered the day he came home to find she'd returned from her parents'. After an awkward greeting he'd looked in the bathroom to see that what had been missing was now in its place in the medicine chest. It was not. With what he was sure was a cool and controlled interrogation, he asked her about her trip. She seemed confused about why he wanted to know exactly where she had been every moment of her trip. Then, knowing he had caught her in the lie, he had, with great flourish and drama, confronted her with the evidence of the missing item.

Of course there was nothing she could say or do in the face of that irrefutable evidence. She had shut down completely and gone to the bedroom in icy silence. The closed door told him to spend the night on the couch. The next morning she was gone before he woke up. When he came home from work that evening, she had been there during the day and taken her clothes and personal items.

Several days later a messenger served him with papers. He thought it odd that she had not given him the opportunity to forgive her, which he knew he would have done.

Now he had to think about reassembling what remained of his life. The divorce was behind him and it bothered him that he had allowed the emotional drain to compromise his standard of life and behavior. The house's condition was a symptom of his personal disarray, and he intended to put things back in order immediately. He wandered the house, taking a mental inventory of the things he must do.

The bedroom was cluttered with clothes tossed around on the floor, on the chair, and hanging off the edges of the bureau. Unfolded laundry was piled on the cedar chest. The bed hadn't been made much less changed since she'd left. He'd start there.

He pulled the bed covers off and tossed them and the pillows towards the door where he could take them down to the laundry room. Then through the space between the headboard and the mattress he made a face at the clumps of dust under the bed. He pulled the bed aside to get under there with the vacuum cleaner.

Then he saw it, laying in a all of dust, a small round half-sphere of rubber with a rounded rim, the device that had allowed them to delay parenthood until they were ready, the missing item that meant she didn't need the pill and he didn't need to use condoms. the object of their most intense disagreement, the catalyst of their breakup.

It was her diaphragm.

Cold Therapy

A large room with its own natural reverb because not much there can absorb sound. Small hazed-over windows on two walls. A florescent light fixture overhead with only one tube working. A circle of seven chairs in the center and men, haggard, care-worn, beat-down men, seated facing one another. Blue jeans and plaid shirts. The occasional baseball cap with pins and insignia. Too warm tonight, thanks to an overworked furnace and a faulty thermostat. One man, younger than the others, out of place in a suit, holding a clipboard, moderating the discussion.

Each man takes his turn and employs as much or as little time as he needs or is willing to need. The member with the floor is maybe early seventies. Unlike the others he wears no emblems, campaign hats marking his tour, medals. He wears jeans and a T-shirt, unmarked. He takes his turn when the man ahead of him breaks down and cries. And he tells his story, the same story as before and to be told again and again for as long as he continues to participate and can remember what he wished he could forget.

He calls attention to the crying man. "You think his tears show weakness, that a real man doesn't cry, that he buries his emotions under a shield of macho? That what you think?" No one responds. They'd heard this before. But he continues, nonetheless, speaking in undertones, emphasizing nothing. "It doesn't work that way."

The moderator interrupts. "Have you ever seen a soldier cry?"

Scoffs. "Hell, yes."

"What, if anything, did you do for him?"

A pause. Then, in a quiet voice, "We were all crying."

Writing something on the clipboard's notepad, "Why were you crying?"

A long pause. "Village... In the jungle... Burned to the ground..." A deep breath. Then rapidly, "Bodies, children, babies, mothers, old people, lying in their blood, riddled with gunfire, punctured by bayonets."

The moderator stops writing and looks up. "My god. Who kills innocent people?"

"We do. We did."

"Can you tell us why?"

He lights a cigarette. Allowed here. "That question has been asked before, even by those of us who were there. It's never been answered."

"Did *you* kill any of the villagers?"

"I was there with the others. By sanctioning what happened, by not speaking out, trying to stop it, we all killed those..." He chokes off the answer.

"But did *you* point a gun, pull a trigger?"

Another pause. "I was an adviser. We had guns, but no role in the combat."

Impatient, almost. "My question is, did you fire that gun?"

He shakes his head and shrugs. "I remember entering the village. I remember afterwards, standing among the carnage, the ruins. I remember only fragments of what happened in between."

Now writing again. "What do you remember?"

"I'd rather not."

"We can't help you if you won't let us in. Tell us about afterwards. How did the others react?"

"Blank stares. In wonder about what we'd just done. Disbelief. Then we cried, to a man. Then we stopped. We didn't speak to one another for days afterward unless it was necessary. We were all somebody nobody wanted to know, to associate with, for what we'd done."

"Did you lose anyone in the skirmish?"

Raised voice. Anger. "What kind of question is that? Of course we lost *someone*! Old ones! Little ones! Helpless ones!"

"Was the real enemy there? Soldiers of the enemy? Were you threatened? Was the killing justified?"

"They were all the enemy." Some of the others nod. They knew.

"Why? Why were women and children the enemy?"

His voice spits venom. "Once, a child walked up to a troop carrier in a convoy. The guys are talking to the little boy, laughing and joking, and then he throws a grenade inside the truck and runs. The grenade didn't go off. He'd forgotten or didn't know to pull the pin. The lieutenant shot the little boy in the back as he ran. He was the enemy. Now he wouldn't kill any of the lieutenant's men. I tell you, they were all the enemy. It's how things were."

The others are affixed to the story. Theirs are horrible too, but none like this one.

"Did you ever shoot a child?" one of them asks.

"I don't know. I advised a lot of young men who no doubt killed civilians in the name of collateral damage. Or whatever it was called back then."

"Back then," the moderator says. "This all happened, what, half a century ago? You've suffered what sounds like immeasurable mental trauma for all those years. Why?"

"Occupational hazard. Part of the job. Comes with the territory. All those other stupid euphemisms we use to keep from saying out loud how it really is."

The moderator leafs through the pages on the clipboard, looking for something. "Did you get help?"

"What help? Talk to people like you, people who have no frame of reference, who can't understand, spill my guts, lay my guilt out on display, ask for exoneration, redemption? What good does that do?"

"Why do you think I can't understand?"

"I was there. I can't understand. How could you? Some of these guys might recognize it. But they don't understand. Nobody does."

"Could it help you to accept that you're not totally to blame?"

"I'm to blame. How can I accept a lie?"

"You didn't put yourself in that village, that gun in your hand."

"So I should blame those who did? They were back here, drawing charts, adding numbers, dictating and disseminating reports. What blame could they assume?"

"They need to share in the blame, don't you think?"

"We all have demons, son. Theirs aren't as big as mine. Deniability from the rear is easy to come by."

"Can you forgive them?"

"I can't forgive myself. Shouldn't that come first?"

"So, if you accept your share of the blame, why do you suppose you can't forgive yourself?"

"How can anyone forgive something that shouldn't be forgiven, that should never have happened? There's no penance for evil." Yet another pause while they wait for him to go on. "I don't know what haunts me more, the looks of terror on the faces of those villagers or the looks of insane rage on our faces. I wish I didn't remember either one. But I shouldn't forget."

"Why not? Why continue to torture yourself?"

"If we forget, it might happen again."

"And a new generation of warriors do not share what you remember, cannot benefit from it?"

"So it will happen again. Can't be avoided."

"Is that what you've learned here?" the moderator asked.

"I haven't learned anything here. Have you?"

Another pointless session over. Nothing conveyed, nothing accomplished. Stories that go in a report. Statistics for yet another chart. He walks alone to the coat rack, puts on his tattered raincoat, goes out into the cold mist, and walks across the dark parking lot to his car.

Also by Al Stevens

http://www.alstevens.com

————————————- Fiction ————————————-

Tommy and Me

Life and Death by Darknet – Darknet #1

Life and Death by Bitcoin – Darknet #2

Life and Death by Drone – Darknet #3

The Resurrection of Beaver Gulch

The Shadow on the Grassy Knoll

Murder at the Old Folks Home

War of the Singularity

Annie Somewhere

Off the Wall Stories

On the Street Where You Die – Stanley Bentworth #1

A Dead Ringer – Stanley Bentworth #2

Clueless: the Pantyhose Slasher Cases - – Stanley Bentworth #3

The Rat Squad – Stanley Bentworth #4

White Collar Murders – Stanley Bentworth #5

Fugitive Warrant – Stanley Bentworth #6

Hooker Stalker Killer Pimp – Stanley Bentworth #7

Murder int the Bermuda Triangle – Stanley Bentworth #8

Assisted Homicide – Stanley Bentworth #9

Corpsicles Cremains – Stanley Bentworth #10

————————————- Nonfiction ————————————-

teach yourself Rhythm Jazz Guitar

teach yourself Jazz Piano Comping

Zen and the Pantser's Muse

Welcome to Programming

teach yourself C++

Ventriloquism: Art, Craft, Profession

Politically Incorrect Scripts for Comedy Ventriloquists

Which One? Confessions of a Closet Ventriloquist

Diabetics Behaving Badly

...and many other computer programming and usage books.

About the Author

Al Stevens is a retired author of computer programming books. For fifteen years he was a senior contributing editor and columnist for Dr. Dobb's Journal, a leading magazine for computer programmers.

Al lives with his wife Judy and a menagerie of cats on Florida's Space Coast where he writes by day and plays piano, string bass, and saxophone by night.

www.ingramcontent.com/pod-product-compliance
Lightning Source LLC
LaVergne TN
LVHW050314160826
845677LV00014B/3394

* 9 7 9 8 6 9 6 9 7 3 4 4 9 *